The wind blew in through a little opening, upon ~~~

And it was a warm wind. A warm wind and a *damp* wind, such as never blows on desert Mars.

Carse squeezed through and stood in the bright day looking outward.

There are times when a man has no emotion, no reaction. Times when all the centers are numbed and the eyes see and the ears hear but nothing communicates itself to the brain, which is protected in this way from madness.

He tried finally to laugh at what he saw though he heard his own laughter as a dry choking cry.

"Mirage, of course," he whispered. "A big mirage. Big as all Mars."

The warm breeze lifted Carse's tawny hair, blew his cloak against him. A cloud drifted over the sun and somewhere a bird screamed harshly. He did not move.

He was looking at an ocean.

It stretched out to the horizon ahead, a vast restlessness of water, milky-white and pale with a shimmering phosphorescence even in daylight.

"Mirage," he said again stubbornly, his reeling mind clinging with the desperation of fear to that one shred of explanation. "It has to be. Because this is still Mars."

Still Mars, still the same planet. The same high hills up into which Penkawr had led him by night.

Or were they the same? Before, the foxhole entrance to the Tomb of Rhiannon had been in a steep cliff-face. Now he stood on the grassy slope of a great hill.

And there were rolling green hills and dark forest down there below him, where before had been only desert. Green hills, green wood and a bright river that ran down a gorge to what had been dead sea-bottom but was now—sea.

Carse's numbed gaze swept along the great coast of the distant shoreline. And down on that far sunlit coast he saw the glitter of a white city and knew that it was Jekkara.

Jekkara, bright and strong between the verdant hills and the mighty ocean, that ocean that had not been seen upon Mars for nearly a million years . . .

Praise for Leigh Brackett

"Leigh took science fiction and lifted it above the genre preconceptions. This is fiction at its most exciting, in the hands of master storyteller."
—*George Lucas, creator of Star Wars and Indiana Jones*

"There's only one Leigh Brackett and there's only one Eric John Stark—both stand alone in their field!"
—*Ray Bradbury*

"Brackett is absolutely at the top of her genre."
—*Publisher's Weekly*

"The Skaith novels share [Edgar Rice Burroughs's] muscular protagonists and headlong pace, but Leigh Brackett's style is head and shoulders above."
—*F. Paul Wilson, author of the Repairman Jack series*

"Leigh Brackett was one of the most influential women writers for the pulps (along with C. L. Moore), her work being an inspiration to Marion Zimmer Bradley, Lin Carter, Jo Clayton, Moorcock and many others."
—*The Encyclopedia of Fantasy*

"Fluid and lovely."
—*Lin Carter*

"Brackett not only continued the great romantic tradition of Edgar Rice Burroughs (though with infinitely more sophistication), but she managed to sneak into the Puritan pulps . . . a sensuousness which the male writers of the period couldn't seem to achieve, both in descriptive ability and hints that the hero and heroine wanted more than for the former to save the latter from a bug-eyed monster . . . Brackett's works are adventurous world-creating at its best."
—*A Reader's Guide to Science Fiction*

"She approached all she wrote with economy and vigor: everything about her early stories—their color, their narrative speed, the brooding forthrightness of their protagonists—made them an ideal and fertile blend of traditional space opera and sword and sorcery."
—*The Encyclopedia of Science Fiction*

THE PLANET STORIES LIBRARY

STRANGE ADVENTURES ON OTHER WORLDS
AVAILABLE MONTHLY EXCLUSIVELY FROM PLANET STORIES!

FOR AUTHOR BIOS AND SYNOPSES,
VISIT PAIZO.COM/PLANETSTORIES

"Martian Elegy" © 2009 by Nicola Griffith

Planet Stories is a division of Paizo Publishing, LLC
2700 Richards Road, Suite 201
Bellevue, WA 98005

PLANET STORIES is a registered trademark of Paizo Publishing, LLC

Visit us online at paizo.com/planetstories

Printed in China

Planet Stories #20, *The Sword of Rhiannon*, by Leigh Brackett

10 9 8 7 6 5 4 3 2 1   2009

The Sword of Rhiannon

by Leigh Brackett

Introduction by Nicola Griffith
Cover by Daren Bader

PLANET STORIES
Seattle
Erik Mona, Publisher

Martian Elegy

BY NICOLA GRIFFITH

The Sword of Rhiannon was first published as "The Sea Kings of Mars" in *Thrilling Wonder Stories*, June 1949: sixty years ago. Leigh Brackett was 33. That year saw the discovery of a moon of Neptune (Nereid), the first flight of a jet-powered airliner, and the debut of the very first local on-air TV station (KDKA-TV in Pittsburgh). The Big Bang theory had been published only the year before—right around the time the United Nations established the World Health Organization, and the arrival of the first shipload of Caribbean immigrants in the UK marked that country's beginnings of multiculturalism.

Earth was changing, growing smaller and more culturally interknit, while the universe was only just beginning to be known. Our understanding of our own solar system was poised on the cusp between the exuberance of frontier imagination and the discipline of science.

Leigh Brackett was born in an era where frontier fiction meant Westerns. As she grew up and began to read, our frontier moved to the inner planets. Earth-bound pulp fiction acquired grit and realism: it became more concerned with urban characters' noirish internal landscapes. But not everyone wanted fiction about what was known. The new frontier fiction—science fiction— looked outwards and upwards.

Artists' impressions of Mars from that time show a twilit world of canyons and drying canals, painted the colour of embers, aching with mystery. Yet all a writer or reader had to do was look up at night, and there it was: tantalizingly real. It couldn't be reached but it could be imagined.

Perhaps the most immediate ancestors of Brackett's Mars fiction are Edgar Rice Burroughs's eleven-novel Barsoom series, starring the mysteriously unchanging John Carter, and C. L. Moore's brilliant stories about Northwest Smith, anti-hero. Both characters are, essentially, assembled from western fiction elements and beamed up to the exotically imagined decadence of ancient Mars. At first glance, Matthew Carse, the protagonist of *Rhiannon*, descends directly from the tall, keen-eyed Carter and Smith. But by the time of *Rhiannon's* first publication, Leigh Brackett had already written her novel-length Chandler *hommage No Good From a Corpse*. She had already written the screenplay for *The Big Sleep* with William Faulkner. It's no surprise, then, that Carse owes as much to hard-boiled crime fiction as to the fantastic adventures of earlier decades.

Matthew Carse, ex-planetary archaeologist, looter and adventurer, is tawny-haired and tall. He carries a proton pistol on his hip and larceny in his heart. His Mars is a desert of dry seas and low canals and cities, such as Jekkara, which were ancient when Ur was a village. In Jekkara of the Low Canals the fumes of *thil* hang in a sweet haze and women and men of ill repute drift through shadowed streets.

Before *Rhiannon*, Brackett might have been reading and writing morally structured noir fiction, but Carse, superficially at least, belongs to the Might Is Right school of action. When a wicked little thief, complaining of Carse's strong-arm tactics, says, "I still don't see why I should give you the lion's share," Carse responds cheerfully, "Because I'm the lion." His attitude to women is . . . interesting. Early in the novel he is a galley slave, enduring a variety of punishments and humiliations (though he never bows his head, not even momentarily—he's a Hero) and he gazes at the arrogant, untouchable Lady Ywain of Sark, who "stood like a dark flame in a nimbus of sunset light." He hates her. He wants to "tame this woman . . . break her utterly, to tear her pride out by the roots and stamp on it." (The reader can't blame him too much: Ywain owns him.) Naturally, by the end of the novel and a long struggle for dominance, they are no longer enemies.

In this sense, *The Sword of Rhiannon* is a romance: the hero is manly, the heroine is proud and untamed—except by the hero, and once they team up nothing can stand before them—and all ends well. It is also a planetary romance in the pulp tradition, a love song and eulogy to a planet: a Mars that never was, where sea kings roamed, mutants were easily classified as Nice (derived from birds and mammals) or Nasty (from reptiles), and, back even farther, lords of forgotten technology once walked the land. The language, too, is often that of pulp fiction—Carse thinks in terms of *grim desire* and the *kiss of the lash*, the heroine's eyes *smoulder* (they might flash, too, though I was too swept up in the story by this time to notice), grins are *wolfish* and all blades are described to excess. It's wonderful.

The Sword of Rhiannon plunges the reader deep into the heart of mystery, that sense of wonder which lies at the heart of the fantastic fiction of the era. In some ways, then, it's old-fashioned, but in others it is not. Carse's journey through space and time epitomises the thoroughly modern notion of the more things change, the more they stay the same. He travels back untold years, to a landscape that, even to a Mars resident and expert, is very nearly unrecognisable. But people are no different: they are engaged in bitter ethnic and national struggles, forgiving and not, pragmatic and unrealistic, dangerous and frightened. However, unlike many of today's careful fictional characters, Brackett's people delight in wild adventure, technology very like magic, and whacking other people's heads off with swords.

Brackett's wonders may be based on the lost science of beings so advanced others think of them as gods, but it is rules-based, not ritualistic. Her work is more than planetary romance: it's surprisingly sophisticated science fiction adventure, with hints of a post-colonial understanding of culture. Just two decades earlier, John Carter was remaking Barsoom to suit himself. Matthew Carse, on the other hand, despite carrying the essence of a god-like Quiru inside him, despite the advantage of futuristic scientific knowledge, despite his size and fabulous physique, can't mould the lost Mars in his image. He finds himself merely one being among many, able to influence but not control long-term social change and political conflict.

Brackett began her career with "Martian Quest," a straight-forward science fiction tale of reason and the laws of nature triumphant, but gradually she began to incorporate not only the political sophistication of mainstream cultural discourse, but her own readings in myth and history.

The proper names of *Rhiannon*—Rhiannon himself, Scyld, Ywain—attest to familiarity with and love for the *Mabinogion*, *Beowulf*, and *Y Gododdin*: the epic poetry of lost peoples. Bracket is an elegiast.

Rhiannon is a hymn to the lost past of a Mars that never was and an elegy for the frontiers that were shrinking every day in the face of sterile data. Twenty years after the novel's first publication, people set foot on the moon. They found nothing but dust. That was a novel Leigh Brackett would never have written.

Nicola Griffith
November, 2008

NICOLA GRIFFITH *is the author of such groundbreaking science fiction and fantasy novels as* Ammonite *and* Slow River. *She has won the Nebula Award for Best Novel; the James Tiptree, Jr. Award; the World Fantasy Award; and an astonishing six Lambda Literary Awards for works exploring LGBT themes.*

The
Sword of
Rhiannon

CHAPTER ONE
The Door to Infinity

MATT CARSE KNEW he was being followed almost as soon as he left Madam Kan's. The laughter of the little dark women was still in his ears and the fumes of *thil* lay like a hot sweet haze across his vision—but they did not obscure from him the whisper of sandaled feet close behind him in the chill Martian night.

Carse quietly loosened his proton-gun in its holster but he did not attempt to lose his pursuer. He did not slow nor quicken his pace as he went through Jekkara.

"The Old Town," he thought. "That will be the best place. Too many people about here."

Jekkara was not sleeping despite the lateness of the hour. The Low Canal towns never sleep, for they lie outside the law and time means nothing to them. In Jekkara and Valkis and Barrakesh night is only a darker day.

Carse walked beside the still black waters in their ancient channel, cut in the dead sea-bottom. He watched the dry wind shake the torches that never went out and listened to the broken music of the harps that were never stilled. Lean lithe men and women passed him in the shadowy streets, silent as cats except for the chime and whisper of the tiny bells the women wear, a sound as delicate as rain, distillate of all the sweet wickedness of the world.

They paid no attention to Carse, though despite his Martian dress he was obviously an Earthman and though an Earthman's life is usually less than the light of a snuffed candle along the Low Canals, Carse was one of them. The men of Jekkara and Valkis and Barrakesh are the aristocracy of thieves and they admire skill and respect knowledge and know a gentleman when they meet one.

That was why Matthew Carse, ex-fellow of the Interplanetary Society of Archaeologists, ex-assistant to the chair of Martian Antiquities at Kahora, dweller on Mars for thirty of his thirty-five years, had been admitted to their far more exclusive society of thieves and had sworn with them the oath of friendship that may not be broken.

Yet now, through the streets of Jekkara, one of Carse's "friends" was stalking him with all the cunning of a sandcat. He wondered momentarily whether the Earth Police Control might have sent an agent here looking for him and immediately discarded that possibility. Agents of anybody's police did not live in Jekkara. No, it was some Low-Canaller on business of his own.

Carse left the canal, turning his back on the dead sea-bottom and facing what had once been inland. The ground rose sharply to the upper cliffs, much gnawed and worn by time and the eternal wind. The old city brooded there, the ancient stronghold of the Sea Kings of Jekkara, its glory long stripped from it by the dropping of the sea.

The New Town of Jekkara, the living town down by the canal, had been old when Ur of the Chaldees was a raw young village. Old Jekkara, with its docks of stone and marble still standing in the dry and dust-choked harbor, was old beyond any Earth conception of the word. Even Carse, who knew as much about it as any living man, was always awed by it.

He chose now to go this way because it was utterly dead and deserted and a man might be alone to talk to his friend.

The empty houses lay open to the night. Time and the scouring wind had worn away their corners and the angles of their doorways, smoothed them into the blurred and weary land. The little low moons made a tangle of conflicting shadows among them. With no effort at all the tall Earthman in his long dark cloak blended into the shadows and disappeared.

Crouched in the shelter of a wall he listened to the footsteps of the man who followed him. They grew louder, quickened, slowed indecisively, then quickened again. They drew abreast, passed and suddenly Carse had moved in a great catlike spring out into the street and a small wiry body was writhing in his grasp, mewing with fright as it shrank from the icy jabbing of the proton-gun in its side.

"No!" it squealed. "Don't! I have no weapon. I mean no harm. I want only to talk to you." Even through the fear a note of cunning crept into the voice. "I have a gift."

Carse assured himself that the man was unarmed and then relaxed his grip. He could see the Martian quite clearly in the moonlight—a ratlike small thief and an unsuccessful one from the worn kilt and harness and the lack of ornaments.

The dregs and sweepings of the Low Canals produced such men as this and they were brothers to the stinging worms that kill furtively out of the dust. Carse did not put his gun away.

"Go ahead," he said. "Talk."

"First," said the Martian, "I am Penkawr of Barrakesh. You may have heard of me." He strutted at the sound of his own name like a shabby bantam rooster.

"No," said Carse. "I haven't."

His tone was like a slap in the face. Penkawr gave a snarling grin.

"No matter. I have heard of you, Carse. As I said, I have a gift for you. A most rare and valuable gift."

"Something so rare and valuable that you had to follow me in the darkness to tell me about it, even in Jekkara." Carse frowned at Penkawr, trying to fathom his duplicity. "Well, what is it?"

"Come and I'll show you."

"Where is it?"

"Hidden. Well hidden up near the palace quays."

Carse nodded. "Something too rare and valuable to be carried or shown even in the thieves' market. You intrigue me, Penkawr. We will go and look at your gift."

Penkawr showed his pointed teeth in the moonlight and led off. Carse followed. He moved lightly, poised for instant action. His gun hand swung loose and ready at his side. He was wondering what sort of price Penkawr of Barrakesh planned to ask for his "gift."

As they climbed upward toward the palace, scrambling over worn reefs and along cliff-faces that still showed the erosion of the sea, Carse had as always the feeling that he was climbing a sort of ladder into the past. It turned him cold with a queer shivering thrill to see the great docks still standing, marked with the mooring of ships. In the eerie moonlight one could almost imagine . . .

"In here," said Penkawr.

Carse followed him into a dark huddle of crumbling stone. He took a little krypton-lamp from his belt pouch and touched it to a glow. Penkawr knelt and scrambled among the broken stones of the floor until he brought forth a long thin bundle wrapped in rags.

With a strange reverence, almost with fear, he began to unwrap it. Carse knelt beside him. He realized that he was holding his breath, watching the Martian's lean dark hands, waiting. Something in the man's attitude had caught him into the same taut mood.

The lamplight struck a spark of deep fire from a half-covered jewel, and then a clean brilliance of metal. Carse leaned forward. Penkawr's eyes, slanted wolf-eyes yellow as topaz, glanced up and caught the Earthman's hard blue gaze, held it for a moment, then shifted away. Swiftly he drew the last covering from the object on the floor.

Carse did not move. The thing lay bright and burning between them and neither man stirred nor seemed even to breathe. The red glow of the lamp painted their faces, lean bone above iron shadows, and the eyes of Matthew Carse were the eyes of a man who looks upon a miracle.

After a long while he reached out and took the thing into his hands. The beautiful and deadly slimness of it, the length and perfect balance, the black hilt and guard that fitted perfectly his large hand, the single smoky jewel that seemed to watch him with a living wisdom, the name etched in most rare and most ancient symbols upon the blade. He spoke, and his voice was no more than a whisper.

"The sword of Rhiannon!"

Penkawr let out his breath in a sharp sigh. "I found it," he said. "I found it."

Carse said, "Where?"

"It does not matter where. I found it. It is yours—for a small price.

"A small price." Carse smiled. "A small price for the sword of a god."

"An evil god," muttered Penkawr. "For more than a million years, Mars has called him the Cursed One."

"I know," Carse nodded. "Rhiannon, the Cursed One, the Fallen One, the rebel one of the gods of long ago. I know the legend, yes. The legend of how the old gods conquered Rhiannon and thrust him into a hidden tomb."

Penkawr looked away. He said, "I know nothing of a tomb."

"You lie," Carse told him softly. "You found the Tomb of Rhiannon or you could not have found his sword. You found, somehow, the key to the oldest sacred legend on Mars. The very stones of that place are worth their weight in gold to the right people."

"I found no tomb," Penkawr insisted sullenly. He went on quickly. "But the sword itself is worth a fortune. I daren't try to sell it—these Jekkarans would snatch it away from me like wolves, if they saw it.

"But you can sell it, Carse." The little thief was shivering in the urgency of his greed. "You can smuggle it to Kahora and sell it to some Earthman for a fortune."

"And I will," Carse nodded. "But first we will get the other things in that tomb."

Penkawr had a sweat of agony on his face. After a long time he whispered, "Leave it at the sword, Carse. That's enough."

It came to Carse that Penkawr's agony was blended of greed and fear. And it was not fear of the Jekkarans but of something else, something that would have to be awesome indeed to daunt the greed of Penkawr.

Carse swore contemptuously. "Are you afraid of the Cursed One? Afraid of a mere legend that time has woven around some old king who's been a ghost for a million years?

He laughed and made the sword flash in the lamplight. "Don't worry, little one. I'll keep the ghosts away. Think of the money. You can have your own palace with a hundred lovely slaves to keep you happy."

He watched fear struggle again with greed in the Martian's face.

"I saw something there, Carse. Something that scared me, I don't know why."

Greed won out. Penkawr licked dry lips. "But perhaps, as you say, it is all only legend. And there are treasures there—even my half share of them would make me wealthy beyond dreams."

"Half?" Carse repeated blandly. "You're mistaken, Penkawr. Your share will be one-third."

Penkawr's face distorted with fury, and he leaped up. "But I found the Tomb! It's my discovery!"

Carse shrugged. "If you'd rather not share that way, then keep your secret to yourself. Keep it—till your 'brothers' of Jekkara tear it from you with hot pincers when I tell them what you've found."

"You'd do that?" choked Penkawr. "You'd tell them and get me killed?"

The little thief stared in impotent rage at Carse, standing tall in the lamp glow with the sword in his hands, his cloak falling back from his naked shoulders, his collar and belt of jewels looted from a dead king flaring. There was no softness in Carse, no relenting. The deserts and the suns of Mars, the cold and the heat and the hunger of them, had flayed away all but the bone and the iron sinew.

Penkawr shivered. "Very well, Carse. I'll take you there—for one-third share."

Carse nodded and smiled. "I thought you would."

Two hours later, they were riding up into the dark timeworn hills that loomed behind Jekkara and the dead sea-bottom.

It was very late now, an hour that Carse loved because it seemed then that Mars was most perfectly itself. It reminded him of a very old warrior, wrapped in a black cloak and holding a broken sword, dreaming the dreams of age which are so close to reality, remembering the sound of trumpets and the laughter and the strength.

The dust of the ancient hills whispered under the eternal wind Phobos had set, and the stars were coldly brilliant. The lights of Jekkara and the great black blankness of the dead sea-bottom lay far behind and below them now. Penkawr led the way up the ascending gorges, their ungainly mounts picking their way with astonishing agility over the treacherous ground.

"This is how I stumbled on the place," Penkawr said. "On a ledge my beast broke its leg in a hole—and the sand widened the hole as it flowed inward, and there was the tomb, cut right into the rock of the cliff. But the entrance was choked when I found it."

He turned and fixed Carse with a sulky yellow stare. "I found it," he repeated. "I still don't see why I should give you the lion's share."

"Because I'm the lion," said Carse cheerfully.

He made passes with the sword, feeling it blend with his flexing wrist, watching the starlight slide down the blade. His heart was beating high with excitement and it was the excitement of the archaeologist as well as of the looter.

He knew better than Penkawr the importance of this find. Martian history is so vastly long that it fades back into a dimness from which only vague legends have come down—legends of human and half-human races, of forgotten wars, of vanished gods.

Greatest of those gods had been the Quiru, hero-gods who were human yet superhuman, who had had all wisdom and power. But there had been a rebel among them—dark Rhiannon, the Cursed One, whose sinful pride had caused some mysterious catastrophe.

The Quiru, said the myths, had for that sin crushed Rhiannon and locked him into a hidden tomb. And for more than a million years men hunted the Tomb of Rhiannon because they believed it held the secrets to Rhiannon's power.

Carse knew too much archaeology to take old legends too seriously. But he did believe that there was an incredibly ancient tomb that had engendered all these myths. And as the oldest relic on Mars it and the things in it would make Matthew Carse the richest man on three worlds—if he lived.

"This way," said Penkawr abruptly. He had ridden in silence for a long time, brooding.

They were far up in the highest hills behind Jekkara. Carse followed the little thief along a narrow ledge on the face of a steep cliff.

Penkawr dismounted and rolled aside a large stone, disclosing a hole in the cliff that was big enough for a man to wriggle through.

"You first," said Carse. "Take the lamp."

Reluctantly Penkawr obeyed, and Carse followed him into the foxhole.

At first there was only an utter darkness beyond the glow of the krypton-lamp. Penkawr slunk, cringing now like a frightened jackal.

Carse snatched the lamp away from him and held it high. They had scrambled through the narrow foxhole into a corridor that led straight back into the cliff. It was square and without ornament, the stone beautifully polished. He started off along it, Penkawr following.

The corridor ended in a vast chamber. It too was square and magnificently plain from what Carse could see of it. There was a dais at one end with an altar of marble, upon which was carved the same symbol that appeared on the hilt of the sword—the *ouroboros* in the shape of a winged serpent. But the circle was broken, the head of the serpent lifted as though looking into some new infinity.

Penkawr's voice came in a reedy whisper from behind his shoulder. "It was here that I found the sword. There are other things around the room but I did not touch them."

Carse had already glimpsed objects ranged around the walls of the great chamber, glittering vaguely through the gloom. He hooked the lamp on his belt and started to examine them.

Here was treasure, indeed! There were suits of mail of the finest workmanship, blazoned with patterns of unfamiliar jewels. There were strangely shaped helmets of unfamiliar glistening metals. A heavy thronelike chair of gold, subtly inlaid in dark metal, had a big tawny gem burning in each armpost.

All these things, Carse knew, were incredibly ancient. They must come from the farthest part of Mars.

"Let us hurry!" Penkawr pleaded.

Carse relaxed and grinned at his own forgetfulness. The scholar in him had for the moment superseded the looter.

"We'll take all we can carry of the smaller jeweled things," he said. "This first haul alone will make us rich."

"But you'll be twice as rich as I," Penkawr said sourly. "I could have got an Earthman in Barrakesh to sell these things for me for a half share only."

Carse laughed. "You should have done so, Penkawr. When you ask for help from a noted specialist you have to pay high fees."

His circuit of the chamber had brought him back to the altar. Now he saw that behind the altar lay a door. He went through it, Penkawr following reluctantly at his heels.

Beyond the doorway was a short passage and at the end of it a door of metal, small and heavily barred. The bars had been lifted, and the door stood open an inch or two. Above it was an inscription in the ancient changeless High Martian characters, which Carse read with practiced ease.

The doom of Rhiannon, dealt unto him forever by the Quiru who are lords of space and time!

Carse pushed the metal door aside and stepped through. And then he stood quite still, looking.

Beyond the door was a great stone chamber as large as the one behind him.

But in this room there was only one thing.

It was a great bubble of darkness. A big, brooding sphere of quivering blackness, through which shot little coruscating particles of brilliance like falling stars seen from another world.

And from this weird bubble of throbbing darkness the lamplight recoiled, afraid.

Something—awe, superstition or some purely physical force—sent a cold tingling shock racing through Carse's body. He felt his hair raising and his flesh seemed to draw away from his bones. He tried to speak and could not, his throat knotted with anxiety and tension.

"This is the thing I told you of," whispered Penkawr. "This is the thing I told you I saw."

Carse hardly heard him. A conjecture so vast that he could not grasp it shook his brain. The scholar's ecstasy was upon him, the ecstasy of discovery that is akin to madness.

This brooding bubble of darkness—it was strangely like the darkness of those blank black spots far out in the galaxy which some scientists have dreamed are holes in the continuum itself, windows into the infinite outside of our universe!

Incredible, surely, and yet that cryptic Quiru inscription—fascinated by the thing, despite its aura of danger, Carse took two steps toward it.

He heard the swift scrape of sandals on the stone floor behind him as Penkawr moved fast. Carse knew instantly that he had blundered in turning his back on the disgruntled little thief. He started to whirl and raise the sword.

Penkawr's thrusting hands jabbed his back before he could complete the movement. Carse felt himself pitched into the brooding blackness.

He felt a terrible rending shock through each atom of his body, and then the world seemed to fall away from him.

"Go share Rhiannon's doom, Earthman! I told you I could get another partner!"

Penkawr's snarling shout came to him from a great distance as he tumbled into a black, bottomless infinity.

CHAPTER TWO

Alien World

CARSE SEEMED TO plunge through a nighted abyss, buffeted by all the shrieking winds of space. An endless, endless fall with the timelessness and the choking horror of a nightmare.

He struggled with the fierce revulsion of an animal trapped by the unknown. His struggle was not physical, for in that blind and screaming nothingness his body was useless. It was a mental fight, the man's inner core of courage reasserting itself, willing itself to stop this nightmare fall through darkness.

And then as he fell, a more terrifying sensation shook him. A feeling that he *was not alone* in this nightmare plunge through infinity, that a dark, strong, pulsating presence was close behind him, grasping for him, groping with eager fingers for his brain.

Carse made a supreme desperate mental effort. His sensation of falling seemed to lessen and then he felt solid rock slipping under his hands and feet. He scrambled frantically forward, in physical effort this time.

He found himself quite suddenly outside the dark bubble again on the floor in the inner chamber of the Tomb.

"What in the Nine Hells . . ." he began shakily and then stopped because the oath seemed so pitifully inadequate for what had happened.

The little krypton-lamp hooked to his belt still cast its reddish glow, the sword of Rhiannon still glittered in his hand.

And the bubble of darkness still gloomed and brooded a foot away from him, flickering with its whirl of diamond motes.

Carse realized that all his nightmare plunging through space had been during the moment he was inside the bubble. What devil's trick of ancient science *was* the thing anyway? Some queer perpetual vortex of force that the mysterious Quiru of long ago had set up, he supposed.

But why had he seemed to fall through infinities inside the thing? And whence had come that terrifying sensation of strong fingers groping eagerly at his brain as he fell?

"A trick of old Quiru science," he muttered shakenly. "And Penkawr's superstitions made him think he could kill me by pushing me into it."

Penkawr? Carse leaped to his feet, the sword of Rhiannon glittering wickedly in his hand.

"Blast his thieving little soul!"

Penkawr was not here now. But he wouldn't have had time to go far. The smile on Carse's face was not pleasant as he went through the doorway.

In the outer chamber he suddenly stopped dead. There were things here now—big strange glittering objects—that had not been here before.

Where had they come from? Had he been longer in that bubble of darkness than he thought? Had Penkawr found these things in hidden crypts and ranged them here to await his return?

Carse's wonder increased as he examined the objects that now loomed amid the mail and other relics he had seen before. These objects did not look like mere art-relics—they looked like carefully fashioned, complicated instruments of unguessable purpose.

The biggest of them was a crystal wheel, the size of a small table, mounted horizontally atop a dull metal sphere. The wheel's rim glistened with jewels cut in precise polyhedrons. And there were other smaller devices of linked crystal prisms and tubes and things built of concentric metal rings and squat looped tubes of massive metal.

Could these glittering objects be the incomprehensible devices of an ancient alien Martian science? That supposition seemed incredible. The Mars of the far past, scholars knew, had been a world of only rudimentary science, a world of sword-fighting sea-warriors whose galleys and kingdoms had clashed on long-lost oceans.

Yet, perhaps, in the Mars of the even *farther* past, there had been a science whose techniques were unfamiliar and unrecognizable?

"But where could Penkawr have found them when we didn't see them before? And why didn't he take any of them with him?"

Memory of Penkawr reminded him that the little thief would be getting farther away every moment. Grimly gripping the sword, Carse turned and hurried down the square stone corridor toward the outer world.

As he strode on Carse became aware that the air in the tomb was now strangely damp. Moisture glistened on the walls. He had not noticed that most un-Martian dampness before and it startled him.

"Probably seepage from underground springs, like those that feed the canals," he thought. "But it wasn't there before."

His glance fell on the floor of the corridor. The drifted dust lay over it thickly as when they had entered. But there were no footprints in it now. No prints at all except those he was now making.

A horrible doubt, a feeling of unreality, clawed at Carse. The un-Martian dampness, the vanishing of their footprints—what had happened to everything in the moment he'd been inside the dark bubble?

He came to the end of the square stone corridor. And it was closed. It was closed by a massive slab of monolithic stone.

Carse stopped, staring at the slab. He fought down his increasing sense of weird unreality and made explanation for himself.

"There must have been a stone door I didn't see—and Penkawr has closed it to lock me in."

He tried to move the slab. It would not budge nor was there any sign of key, knob or hinge.

Finally Carse stepped back and leveled his proton-pistol. Its hissing streak of atomic flame crackled in the rock slab, searing and splitting it.

The slab was thick. He kept the tripper of his gun depressed for minutes. Then, with a hollowly reverberating crash the fragments of the split slab fell back in toward him.

But beyond, instead of the open air, there lay a solid mass of dark red soil.

"The whole Tomb of Rhiannon—buried, now; Penkawr must have started a cave-in."

Carse didn't believe that. He didn't believe it at all but he tried to make himself believe, for he was becoming more and more afraid. And the thing of which he was afraid was impossible.

With blind anger he used the flaming beam of the pistol to undercut the mass of soil that blocked his way. He worked outward until the beam suddenly died as the charge of the gun ran out. He flung away the useless pistol and attacked the hot smoking mass of soil with the sword.

Panting, dripping, his mind a whirl of confused speculations, he dug outward through the soft soil till a small hole of brilliant daylight opened in front of him.

Daylight? Then he'd been in the weird bubble of darkness longer than he had imagined.

The wind blew in through a little opening, upon his face. And it was a warm wind. A warm wind and a *damp* wind, such as never blows on desert Mars.

Carse squeezed through and stood in the bright day looking outward.

There are times when a man has no emotion, no reaction. Times when all the centers are numbed and the eyes see and the ears hear but nothing communicates itself to the brain, which is protected in this way from madness.

He tried finally to laugh at what he saw though he heard his own laughter as a dry choking cry.

"Mirage, of course," he whispered. "A big mirage. Big as all Mars."

The warm breeze lifted Carse's tawny hair, blew his cloak against him. A cloud drifted over the sun and somewhere a bird screamed harshly. He did not move.

He was looking at an ocean.

It stretched out to the horizon ahead, a vast restlessness of water, milky-white and pale with a shimmering phosphorescence even in daylight.

"Mirage," he said again stubbornly, his reeling mind clinging with the desperation of fear to that one shred of explanation. "It has to be. Because this is still Mars."

Still Mars, still the same planet. The same high hills up into which Penkawr had led him by night.

Or were they the same? Before, the foxhole entrance to the Tomb of Rhiannon had been in a steep cliff-face. Now he stood on the grassy slope of a great hill.

And there were rolling green hills and dark forest down there below him, where before had been only desert. Green hills, green wood and a bright river that ran down a gorge to what had been dead sea-bottom but was now—sea.

Carse's numbed gaze swept along the great coast of the distant shoreline. And down on that far sunlit coast he saw the glitter of a white city and knew that it was Jekkara.

Jekkara, bright and strong between the verdant hills and the mighty ocean, that ocean that had not been seen upon Mars for nearly a million years.

Matthew Carse knew then that it was no mirage. He sat and hid his face in his hands. His body was shaken by deep tremors and his nails bit into his own flesh until blood trickled down his cheeks.

He knew now what had happened to him in that vortex of darkness, and it seemed to him that a cold voice repeated a certain warning inscription in tones of distant thunder.

"The Quiru are lords of space and time—of *time*—OF TIME!"

Carse, staring out over the green hills and the milky ocean, made a terrible effort to grapple with the incredible.

I have come into the past of Mars. All my life I have studied and dreamed of that past. Now I am in it. I, Matthew Carse, archaeologist, renegade, looter of tombs.

"The Quiru for their own reasons built a way and I came through it. Time is to us the unknown dimension but the Quiru knew it!"

Carse had studied science. You had to know the elements of a half-dozen sciences to be a planetary archaeologist. He frantically ransacked memory now for an explanation.

Had his first guess about that bubble of darkness been right? Was it really a hole in the continuum of the universe? If that were so he could dimly understand what had happened to him.

For the space-time continuum of the universe was finite, limited. Einstein and Riemann had proved that long ago. And he had fallen clear out of that continuum and then back into it again— but into a different time-frame from his own.

What was it that Kaufman had once written? "The Past is the Present-that-exists-at-a-distance." He had come back into that other distant Present, that was all. There was no reason to be afraid.

But he was afraid. The horror of that nightmare transition to this green and smiling Mars of long ago wrenched a gusty cry from his lips.

Blindly, still gripping the jeweled sword, he leaped up and turned to re-enter the buried Tomb of Rhiannon.

"I can go back the way I came, back through that hole in the continuum."

He stopped a convulsive shudder running through his frame. He could not make himself face again that bubble of glittering gloom, that dreadful plunge through inter-dimensional infinity.

He dared not. He had not the Quiru's wisdom. In that perilous plunge across time mere chance had flung him into this past age. He could not count on chance to return him to his own far-future age.

"I'm here," he said. "I'm here in the distant past of Mars and I'm here to stay."

He turned back around and gazed out again upon that incredible vista. He stayed there a long time, unmoving. The sea birds came and looked at him and flashed away on their sharp white wings. The shadows lengthened.

His eyes swung again to the white towers of Jekkara down in the distance, queenly in the sunlight above the harbor. It was not the Jekkara he knew, the thieves' city of the Low Canals, rotting away into dust, but it was a link to the familiar and Carse desperately needed such a link.

He would go to Jekkara. And he would try not to think. He must not think at all or surely his mind would crack.

Carse gripped the haft of the jeweled sword and started down the grassy slope of the hill.

CHAPTER THREE
City of the Past

IT WAS A long way to the city. Carse moved at a steady plodding pace. He did not try to find the easiest path but rammed his way through and over all obstacles, never deviating from the straight line that led to Jekkara. His cloak hampered him and he tore it off. His face was empty of all expression, but sweat ran down his cheeks and mingled with the salt of tears.

He walked between two worlds. He went through valleys drowsing in the heat of the summer day, where leafy branches of strange trees raked his face and the juice of crushed grasses stained his sandals. Life, winged and furred and soft of foot, fled from him with a stir and rustle. And yet he knew that he walked in a desert, where even the wind had forgotten the names of the dead for whom it mourned.

He crossed the high ridges, where the sea lay before him and he could hear the boom of the surf on the beaches. And yet he saw only a vast dead plain, where the dust ran in little wavelets among the dry reefs. The truths of thirty years' living are not easily forgotten.

The sun sank slowly toward the horizon. As Carse topped the last ridge above the city and started down he walked under a vault of flame. The sea burned as the white phosphorescence took color from the clouds. With dazed wonder Carse saw the gold and crimson and purple splash down the long curve of the sky and run out over the water.

He could look down upon the harbor. The docks of marble that he had known so well, worn and cracked by ages and whelmed by desert sand, lying lonely beneath the moons. The same docks, and yet now, mirage-like, the seas filled the basin of the harbor.

Round-hulled trading ships lay against the quays and the shouts of stevedores and sweating slaves rose up to him on the evening air. Shallops came and went amid the ships and out beyond the breakwater he saw the fishing fleet of Jekkara coming home with sails of cinnabar dark against the west.

By the palace quays, near the very spot where he had gone with Penkawr to see the sword of Rhiannon, a long lean dark war-galley with a brazen ram crouched like a sullen black panther. Beyond it were other galleys. And above them, tall and proud, the white towers of the palace rose.

"I have come far back into the past of Mars indeed! For this is the Mars of a million years ago that archaeology has always pictured!"

A planet of conflicting civilizations which had developed little science yet which cherished a legend of the super-science of the great Quiru who had been before even this time.

"A planet of the lost past that God's law intended no man of my own time ever to see!"

Matthew Carse shivered as though it were very cold. Slowly, slowly, he went down into the streets of Jekkara and it seemed to him, in the sunset, that the whole city was stained with blood.

The walls closed him in. There was a mist before his eyes and roaring in his ears but he was aware of people. Lean lithe men and women who passed him in the narrow ways, who jostled against him and went on, then stopped and turned to stare. The dark and catlike people of Jekkara, Jekkara of the Low Canals and of this other age.

He heard the music of the harps and the chiming whisper of the little bells the women wore. The wind touched his face but it was a moist wind and warm, heavy with the breath of the sea, and it was more than a man could bear.

Carse went on but he had no idea where he was going or what he had to do. He went on only because he was already moving and had not the wit to stop.

One foot before the other, stolid, blind, like a man bewitched, he walked through the streets among the dark Jekkarans, a tall blond man trailing a naked sword.

The people of the city watched him. People of the harborside, of the wine shops and twisting alleys. They drew away before and closed in behind, following and staring at him.

The gap of ages lay between them. His kilt was of strange cloth, an unknown dye. His ornaments were of a time and country they would never see. And his face was alien.

This very alienage held them back for a time. Some breath of the incredible truth clung to him and made them afraid. Then someone said a name and someone else repeated it and in the space of a few seconds there was no more mystery, no more fear—only hate.

Carse heard the name. Dimly, from a great distance, he heard it as it grew from a whisper into a howling cry that ran wolf-like through the streets.

"Khond! Khond! A spy from Khondor!" And then another word. "*Slay!*"

The name of "Khond" meant nothing to Carse, but he recognized it for what it was, an epithet and a curse. The voice of the mob carried to him the warning of death and he tried to rouse himself for the instinct of survival is strong. But his brain was numbed and would not wake.

A stone struck him on the cheek. The physical shock brought him to a little. Blood ran into his mouth. The salt-sweet taste of it told him the destruction had already begun. He tried to shake the dark veils aside, far enough at least to see the enemy that threatened him.

He had come out into an open space by the docks. Now, in the twilight, the sea flamed with cold white fire. Masts of the moored ships stood black against it. Phobos was rising, and in the mingled light Carse saw that there were creatures climbing into the rigging of the ships and that they were furred and chained and not wholly human.

And he saw on the wharfside two slender white-skinned men with wings. They wore the loin cloth of the slave and their wings were broken.

The square was filled with people. More of them poured in from the narrow alley-mouths, drawn by the shout of *Spy!* It echoed from the buildings and the name of "Khondor" hammered at him.

From the wharfside, from the winged slaves and the chained creatures of the ships, a fervent cry reached him.

"Hail, Khondor! Fight, Man!"

Women screamed like harpies. Another stone whistled past his ear. The mob surged and jostled but those nearest Carse held back, wary of the great jeweled sword with its shining blade.

Carse shouted. He swung the sword in a humming arc around him and the Jekkarans, who had shorter blades, melted back.

Again from the wharfside he heard, "Hail, Khondor! Down with the Serpent, down with Sark! Fight, Khond!"

He knew that the slaves would have helped him if they could.

One part of his mind was beginning to function now—the part that had to do with a long experience in saving his own neck. He was only a few paces away from the buildings at his back. He whirled and leaped suddenly, the bright steel swinging.

It bit twice into flesh and then he had gained the doorway of a ship's chandler, so that they could only come at him from the front. A small advantage but every second a man could stay alive was a second gained.

He made a flickering barrier of steel before him and then bellowed, in their own High Martian. "Wait! I am no Khond!"

The crowd broke into jeering laughter.

"He says he is not of Khondor!"

"Your own friends hail you, Khond! Hark to the Swimmers and the Skyfolk!"

Carse cried, "No! I am not of Khondor. I am not—" He stopped short. He had almost said he was not of Mars.

A green-eyed girl, hardly more than a child, darted almost into the circle of death he wove before him. Her teeth showed white as a rat's.

"Coward!" she screamed. "Fool! Where but in Khondor do they breed men like you, with pale hair and sickly skin? Where else could you be from, oh clumsy thing with the barbarous speech?"

Something of the strange look returned to Carse's face and he said, "I am from Jekkara."

They laughed. They shrieked with laughter until the square rocked with it. Now they had lost all awe of him. His every word stamped him as what the girl had called him, a coward and a fool. Almost contemptuously, they attacked.

This was real enough to Carse, this mass of hate-filled faces and wicked short-swords coming at him. He struck out ragingly with the long sword of Rhiannon, his rage less against this murderous rabble than against the fate that had pitchforked him into their world.

Several of them died on the jeweled sword and the rest drew back. They stood glaring at him like jackals who have trapped a wolf. Then through their hissing came an exultant cry.

"The Sark soldiers are coming! They'll cut down this Khond spy for us!"

Carse, backed against a locked door and panting, saw a little phalanx of black-mailed, black-helmeted warriors pushing through the rabble like a ship through waves.

They were coming straight toward him and the Jekkarans were already yelling in eager anticipation of the kill.

CHAPTER FOUR

Perilous Secret

THE DOOR AGAINST which Carse's back was braced suddenly gave way, opening inward. He reeled backward into the black interior.

As he staggered for balance the door suddenly slammed shut again. He heard a bar fall and then a low, throaty chuckle from beside him.

"That will hold them for a while. But we'd better get out of here quickly, Khond. Those Sark soldiers will cut the door open."

Carse swung around, his sword raised, but was blind in the darkness of the room. He could smell rope and tar and dust but could see nothing.

A frantic hammering began outside the door. Then Carse's eyes, becoming accustomed to the obscurity, made out a ponderous corpulent figure close behind him.

The man was big, fleshy and soft looking, a Martian who wore a kilt that looked ridiculously scanty on his fat figure. His face was moonlike, creased and crinkled in a reassuring grin as his small eyes looked unfearingly at Carse's raised sword.

"I'm no Jekkaran or Sark either," he said reassuringly. "I'm Boghaz Hoi of Valkis and I've my own reasons for helping any man of Khond. But we'll have to go quickly."

"Go where?"

Carse had to drag the words out, he was still breathing so painfully.

"To a place of safety." The other paused as new louder hammering began upon the door. "That's the Sarks. I'm leaving. Come or stay as you like, Khond."

He turned toward the back of the dark room, moving with astonishing lightness and ease for one so corpulent. He did not look back to see if Carse was following.

But there was really no choice for Carse. Half-dazed as he still was he was of no mind to face the eruption of those mailed soldiers and the Jekkaran rabble. He followed Boghaz Hoi.

The Valkisian chuckled as he squeezed his bulk through a small open window at the rear of the room.

"I know every rathole in this harbor quarter. That's why, when I saw you backed against old Taras Thur's door, I simply went around through and let you in. Snatched you from under their noses."

"But why?" Carse asked again.

"I told you—I have a sympathy for Khonds. They're men enough to snap their fingers at Sark and the damned Serpent. I help one when I can."

It didn't make sense to Carse. But how could it? How could he know anything of the hates and passions of this Mars of the remote past?

He was trapped in this strange Mars of long ago and he had to grope his way in it like an ignorant child. It was certain that the mob out there had tried to kill him.

They had taken him for a Khond. Not the Jekkaran rabble alone but those strange slaves—the semi-humans with the broken wings, the furred sleek chained creatures who had cheered him from the galleys.

Carse shivered. Until now, he had been too dazed to think of the strangeness of those not-quite-human slaves.

And who were the Khonds?

"This way," Boghaz Hoi interrupted his thoughts.

They had treaded a shadowy little labyrinth of stinking alleys and the fat Valkisian was squeezing though a narrow door into the dark interior of a little hut.

Carse followed him inside. He heard the whistle of the blow in the dark and tried to dodge but there was no time.

The concussion exploded, a bomb of stars inside his head and he felt the rough floor grinding his face.

He awoke with flickering light in his eyes. There was a small bronze lamp burning on a stool close to him. He was lying on the dirt floor of the hut. When he tried to move he found that his wrists and ankles were bound to pegs driven into the packed earth.

Sickening pain racked his head and he sank back. There was a rustle of movement and Boghaz Hoi crouched down beside him. The Valkisian's moonface was expressive of sympathy as he held a clay cup of water to Carse's lips.

"I struck too hard I'm afraid. But then, in the dark with an armed man, one has to be careful. Do you feel like talking now?"

Carse looked up at him and old habit made him control the rage that shook him. "About what?" he asked.

Boghaz said, "I am a frank and truthful man. When I saved you from the mob out there my only idea was to rob you."

Carse saw that his jeweled belt and collar had been transferred to Boghaz, who wore them both around his neck. The Valkisian now raised a plump hand and fingered them lovingly.

"Then," he continued, "I got a closer look—at that." He nodded toward the jeweled sword that leaned against the stool, shimmering in the lamplight. "Now, many men would examine it and see only a handsome sword. But I, Boghaz, am a man of education. I recognized the symbols on that blade."

He leaned forward. "Where did you get it?"

A warning instinct made Carse lie readily. "I bought it from a trader."

Boghaz shook his head. "No you didn't. There are spots of corrosion on the blade, scales of dust in the carvings. The hilt has not been polished. No trader would sell it in that condition.

"No, my friend, that sword has lain a long time in the dark, in the tomb of him who owned it—the tomb of Rhiannon."

Carse lay without moving, looking at Boghaz. He did not like what he saw.

The Valkisian had a kind and merry face. He would be excellent company over a bottle of wine. He would love a man like a brother and regret exceedingly the necessity of cutting out his heart.

Carse schooled his expression into sullen blankness. "It may be Rhiannon's sword for all I know. Nevertheless, I bought it from a trader."

The mouth of Boghaz, which was small and pink, puckered and he shook his head. He reached out and patted Carse's cheek.

"Please don't lie to me, friend. It upsets me to be lied to."

"I'm not lying," Carse said. "Listen—you have the sword. You have my ornaments. You have all you can get out of me. Just be satisfied."

Boghaz sighed. He looked down appealingly at Carse. "Have you no gratitude? Didn't I save your life?"

Carse said sardonically, "It was a noble gesture."

"It was. It was indeed. If I'm caught for it my life won't be worth that." He snapped his fingers. "I cheated the mob of a moment's pleasure and it wouldn't do a bit of good to tell them that you really aren't a Khond at all."

He let that fall very casually but he watched Carse shrewdly from under his fat eyelids.

Carse looked back at him, hard-eyed, and his face showed nothing.

"What gave you that idea?"

Boghaz laughed. "No Khond would be ass enough to show his face in Jekkara to begin with. And especially if he'd found the lost secret all Mars has hunted for an age—the secret of the Tomb of Rhiannon."

Carse's face moved no muscle but he was thinking swiftly. So the Tomb was a lost mystery in this time as in his own future time?

He shrugged. "I know nothing of Rhiannon or his Tomb."

Boghaz squatted down on the floor beside Carse and smiled down at him like one humoring a child who wishes to play.

"My friend, you are not being honest with me. There's no man on Mars who doesn't know that the Quiru long, long ago left our world because of what Rhiannon, the Cursed One among them, had done. And all men know they built a secret tomb before they left, in which they locked Rhiannon and his powers.

"Is it wonderful that men should covet the powers of the gods? Is it strange that ever since men have hunted that lost Tomb? And now that you have found it, do I, Boghaz, blame you for wanting to keep the secret to yourself?"

He patted Carse's shoulder and beamed.

"It is but natural on your part. But the secret of the Tomb is too big for you to handle. You need my brains to help you. Together, with that secret, we can take what we want of Mars."

Carse said without emotion. "You're crazy. I have no secret. I bought the sword from a trader."

Boghaz stared at him for a long moment. He stared very sadly. Then he sighed heavily.

"Think, my friend. Wouldn't it be better to tell me than to make me force it out of you?"

"There's nothing to tell," Carse said harshly.

He did not wish to be tortured. But that odd warning instinct had returned more strongly. Something deep within him warned him not to tell the secret of the Tomb!

And anyway, even if he told, the fat Valkisian was likely to kill him then to prevent him from telling anyone else the secret.

Boghaz sorrowfully shrugged fat shoulders. "You force me to extreme measures. And I hate that. I'm too chicken-hearted for this work. But if it's necessary—"

He was reaching into his belt-pouch for something when suddenly both men heard a sound of voices in the alleyway outside and the tramp of heavily shod feet.

Outside, a voice cried, "*There!* That is the sty of the Boghaz hog!"

A fist began to hammer on the door with such force that the small room rang like the inside of a drum.

"Open up, there, fat scum of Valkis!"

Heavy shoulders began to heave against the door.

"Gods of Mars!" groaned Boghaz. "That Sark press-gang has tracked us down!"

He grabbed the sword of Rhiannon and was in the act of hiding it in his bed when the warped planks of the door gave under the tremendous beating, and a spate of armed men burst into the room.

CHAPTER FIVE

Slave of Sark

BOGHAZ RECOVERED HIMSELF with magnificent aplomb. He bowed deeply to the leader of the press-gang, a huge black-bearded, hawk-nosed man wearing the same black mail that Carse had seen on the Sark soldiers in the square.

"My lord Scyld!" said Boghaz. "I regret that I am corpulent, and therefore slow of motion. I would not for worlds have given your lordship the trouble of breaking my poor door, especially"—his face beamed with the light of pure innocence—"especially as I was about to set out in search of you."

He gestured toward Carse.

"I have him for you, you see," he said. "I have him safe."

Scyld set his fists on his hips, thrust his spade beard up into the air and laughed. Behind him the soldiers of the press-gang took it up and, behind them, the rabble of Jekkarans who had come to see the fun.

"He has him safe," said Scyld, "for us."

More laughter.

Scyld stepped closer to Boghaz. "I suppose," he said, "that it was your loyalty that prompted you to spirit this Khond dog away from my men in the first place."

"My lord," protested Boghaz, "the mob would have killed him."

"That's why my men went in—we wanted him alive. A dead Khond is of no use to us. But you had to be helpful Boghaz. Fortunately you were seen." He reached out and fingered the stolen ornaments that Boghaz wore around his neck. "Yes," said Scyld, "very fortunate."

He wrenched the collar and the belt away, admired the play of light on the jewels and dropped them into his belt-pouch. Then he moved to the bed, where the sword lay half-concealed among the blankets. He picked it up, felt the weight and balance of the blade, examined casually the chasing on the steel and smiled.

"A real weapon," he said. "Beautiful as the Lady herself—and just as deadly."

He used the point to cut Carse free of his bonds.

"Up, Khond," he said, and helped him with the toe of his heavy sandal.

Carse staggered to his feet and shook his head once to clear it. Then, before the men of the press-gang could grasp him, he smashed his hard fist savagely into the expansive belly of Boghaz.

Scyld laughed. He had a deep, hearty seaman's laugh. He kept guffawing as his soldiers pulled Carse away from the doubled-up gasping Valkisian.

"No need for that now," Scyld told him. "There's plenty of time. You two are going to see a lot of each other."

Carse watched a horrible realization break over the fat face of Boghaz.

"My lord," quavered the Valkisian, still gasping. "I am a loyal man. I wish only to serve the interests of Sark and her Highness, the Lady Ywain." He bowed.

"Naturally," said Scyld. "And how could you better serve both Sark and the Lady Ywain than by pulling an oar in her war-galley?"

Boghaz was losing color by the second. "But, my lord—"

"What?" cried Scyld fiercely. "You protest? Where is your loyalty, Boghaz?" He raised the sword. "You know what the penalty is for treason."

The men of the press-gang were near to bursting with suppressed laughter.

"Nay," said Boghaz hoarsely. "I am loyal. No one can accuse me of treason. I wish only to serve—" He stopped short, apparently realizing that his own tongue had trapped him neatly.

Scyld brought the flat of the blade down in a tremendous thwack across Boghaz' enormous buttocks.

"Go then and serve!" he shouted.

Boghaz leaped forward, howling. The press-gang grabbed him. In a few seconds they had shackled him and Carse securely together.

Scyld complacently thrust the sword of Rhiannon into his own sheath after tossing his own blade to a soldier to carry. He led the way swaggeringly out of the hut.

Once again, Carse made a pilgrimage through the streets of Jekkara but this time by night and in chains, stripped of his jewels and his sword.

It was to the palace quays they went, and the cold shivering thrill of unreality came again upon Carse as he looked at the high towers ablaze with light and the soft white fire of the sea that glowed far out in the darkness.

The whole palace quarter swarmed with slaves, with men-at-arms in the sable mail of Sark, with courtiers and women and jongleurs. Music and the sounds of revelry came from the palace itself as they passed beneath it.

Boghaz spoke to Carse in a rapid undertone. "The blockheads didn't recognize that sword. Keep quiet about your secret—or they'd take us both to Caer Dhu for questioning and you know what *that* means!" He shuddered over all his great body.

Carse was too numbed to answer. Reaction from this incredible world and from sheer physical fatigue was sweeping over him like a wave.

Boghaz continued loudly for the benefit of their guards. "All this splendor is in honor of the Lady Ywain of Sark. A princess as great as her father, King Garach! To serve in *her* galley will be a privilege."

Scyld laughed mockingly. "Well said, Valkisian! And your fervent loyalty shall be rewarded. That privilege will be yours a long time."

The black war-galley loomed up before them, their destination. Carse saw that it was long, rakish, with a rowers' pit splitting its deck down the middle and a low stern-castle aft.

Flamboys were blazing on the low poop deck back there and ruddy light spilled from the windows of the cabins beneath it. Sark soldiers clustered back there, chaffing each other loudly.

But in the long dark rowers' pit there was only a bitter silence.

Scyld raised his bull voice in a shout. "Ho, there, Callus!"

A large man came trunting out of the shadowy pit, negotiating the catwalk with practiced skill. His right hand clutched a leathern bottle and his left a black whip—a long-lashed thing, supple from much using.

He saluted Scyld with the bottle, not troubling to speak.

"Fodder for the benches," Scyld said. "Take them." He chuckled. "And see that they're chained to the same oar."

Callus looked at Carse and Boghaz, then smiled lazily and gestured with the bottle, "Get aft, carrion," he grunted and let the lash run out.

Carse glared at him out of red eyes and snarled. Boghaz gripped the Earthman by the shoulder and shook him.

"Come on, fool!" he said. "We'll get enough beatings without you asking for them."

He pulled Carse with him, down into the rowers' pit and forward along the catwalk between the benches.

The Earthman, numbed by shock and exhaustion, was only dimly aware of faces turned to watch them, of the mutter of chains and the smell of bilges. He only half saw the round curious heads of the two furry creatures who slept on the catwalk and who moved to let them pass.

The last starboard bench facing the stern-castle had only one sleeping man chained to its oar, its other two places being empty. The press-gang stood by until Carse and Boghaz were safely chained.

Then they went off with Scyld. Callus cracked his whip with a sound like a gunshot, apparently as a reminder to all hands, and went forward.

Boghaz nudged Carse in the ribs. Then he leaned over and shook him. But Carse was beyond caring what Boghaz had to say. He was sound asleep, doubled over the loom of the oar.

Carse dreamed. He dreamed that he was again taking that nightmare plunge through the shrieking infinities of the dark bubble in Rhiannon's tomb. He was falling, falling—

And again he had that sensation of a strong, living presence close beside him in the awful plunge, of something grasping at his brain with a dark and dreadful eagerness.

"No!" Carse whispered in his dream. *"No!"*

He husked that refusal again—a refusal of something that the dark presence was asking him to do, something veiled and frightful.

But the pleading became more urgent, more insistent, and whatever it was that pleaded seemed now far stronger than in the Tomb of Rhiannon. Carse uttered a shuddering cry.

"No, Rhiannon!"

He found himself suddenly awake, looking dazedly along the moonlit oar-bank.

Callus and the overseer were striding along the catwalk, lashing the slaves to wakefulness. Boghaz was looking at Carse with a strange expression.

"You cried out to the Cursed One!" he said.

The other slave at their oar was staring at him too and so were the luminous eyes of the two furry shadows chained to the catwalk.

"A bad dream," Carse muttered. "That was all."

He was interrupted by a whistle and a crack and a searing pain along his back.

"Stand to your oar, carrion!" roared Callus' voice from above him.

Carse voiced a tigerish cry but Boghaz instantly stopped his mouth with one big paw. "Steady!" he warned. "Steady!"

Carse got hold of himself but not in time to avoid another stroke of the whip. Callus stood grinning down at him.

"You'll want care," he said. "Care, and watching."

Then he lifted his head and yelled along the oarbank.

"All right, you scum, you carrion! Sit up to it! We're starting on the tide for Sark and I'll flay alive the first man who loses a stroke!"

Overhead seamen were busy in the rigging. The sails fell wide from the yards, dark in the moonlight.

There was a sudden pregnant silence along the shop, a drawing of breath and tightening of sinews. On a platform at the end of the catwalk a slave crouched ready over a great hide drum.

An order was given. The fist of the drummer clenched and fell.

All along the oar-bank the great sweeps shot out, found water, bit and settled to a steady rhythm. The drumbeat gave the time and the lash enforced it. Somehow Carse and Boghaz managed to do what they had to do.

The rowers' pit was too deep for sight, except what one could glimpse through the oar ports. But Carse heard the full-throated cheer of the crowd on the quays as the war-galley of Ywain and Sark cleared the slip, standing out into the open harbor.

The night breeze was light and the sails drew little. The drum picked up the beat, drove it faster, sent the long sweeps swinging and set the scarred and sweating backs of the slaves to their full stretch and strain.

Carse felt the lift of the hull to the first swell of the open sea. Through the oar port, he glimpsed a heaving ocean of milky flame. He was bound for Sark across the White Sea of Mars.

CHAPTER SIX

On the Martian Sea

THE GALLEY RAISED a fair breeze at last and the slaves were allowed to rest. Again Carse slept. When he awoke for the second time it was dawn.

Through the oar port he watched the sea change color with the sunrise. He had never seen anything so ironically beautiful. The water caught the pale tints of the first light and warmed them with its own phosphorescent fire—amethyst and pearl and rose and saffron. Then, as the sun rose higher, the sea changed to one sheet of burning gold.

Carse watched until the last color had faded, leaving the water white again. He was sorry when it was all gone. It was unreal and he could pretend that he was still asleep, in Madam Kan's on the Low Canal, dreaming the dreams that come with too much *thil*.

Boghaz snored untroubled by his side. The drummer slept beside his drum. The slaves dropped over the oars, resting.

Carse looked at them. They were a vicious, hard-bitten lot—mostly convicted criminals, he supposed. He thought he could recognize Jekkaran, Valkisian and Keshi types.

But a few of them, like the third man at his own oar, were of a different breed. Khonds, he supposed, and he could see why he had been mistaken for one of them. They were big raw-boned men with light eyes and fair or ruddy hair and a barbarian look that Carse liked.

His gaze dropped to the catwalk and he saw clearly now the two creatures who lay shackled there. The same breed as those who had cheered him up in the square last night, from the wharfside ships.

They were not human. Not quite. They were kin to the seal and the dolphin, to the strong perfect loveliness of a cresting wave. Their bodies were covered with sort dark fur, thinning to a fine down on the face. Their features were delicately cut, handsome.

They rested but did not sleep and their eyes were open, large and dark and full of intelligence.

These, he guessed, were what the Jekkarans had referred to as Swimmers. He wondered what their function was, aboard ship. One was a man, the other a woman. He could not, somehow, think of them as merely male and female like beasts.

He realized that they were studying him with fixed curiosity. A small shiver ran over him. There was something uncanny about their eyes, as though they could see beyond ordinary horizons.

The woman spoke in a soft voice. "Welcome to the brotherhood of the lash."

Her tone was friendly. Yet he sensed in it a certain reserve, a note of puzzlement.

Carse smiled at her. "Thanks."

Again, he was conscious that he spoke the old High Martian with an accent. It was going to be a problem to explain his race, for he knew that the Khonds themselves would not make the same mistake the Jekkarans had.

The next words of the Swimmer convinced him of that.

"You are not of Khondor," she said, "though you resemble its people. What is your country?"

A man's rough voice joined in. "Yes, what is it, stranger?"

Carse turned to see that the big Khond slave, who was third man on his oar, was eyeing him with hostile suspicion.

The man went on. "Word went round that you were a captured Khond spy but that's a lie. More likely you're a Jekkaran masquerading as a Khond, set here among us by the Sarks."

A low growl ran through the oar bank.

Carse had known he would have to account for himself somehow and had been thinking quickly. Now he spoke up.

"I'm no Jekkaran but a tribesman from far beyond Shun. From so far that all this is like a new world to me."

"You might be," the big Khond conceded grudgingly. "You've got a queer look and way of talking. What brought you and this hog of Valkis aboard?"

Boghaz was awake now and the fat Valkisian answered hastily. "My friend and I were wrongfully accused of theft by the Sarks! The shame of it—I, Boghaz of Valkis, convicted of pilfering! An outrage on justice!"

The Khond spat disgustedly and turned away. "I thought so."

Presently Boghaz found an opportunity to whisper to Carse. "They think now we're a pair of condemned thieves. Best let them think so, my friend."

"What are you but that?" Carse retorted brutally.

Boghaz studied him with shrewd little eyes. "What are *you*, friend?"

"You heard me—I come from far beyond Shun."

From beyond Shun and from beyond this whole world, Carse thought grimly. But he couldn't tell these people the incredible truth about himself.

The fat Valkisian shrugged. "If you wish to stick to that it's all right with me. I trust you implicitly. Are we not partners?"

Carse smiled sourly at that ingenuous question. There was something about the impudence of this fat thief which he found amusing.

Boghaz detected his smile. "Ah, you are thinking of my unfortunate violence toward you last night. It was mere impulsiveness. We shall forget it. I, Boghaz, have already forgotten it," he added magnanimously.

"The fact remains that you, my friend, possess the secret of"—he lowered his voice to a murmur—"of the Tomb of Rhiannon. It's lucky that Scyld was too ignorant to recognize the sword! For that secret, rightly exploited, can make us the biggest men on Mars!"

Carse asked him, "Why is the Tomb of Rhiannon so important?"

The question took Boghaz off guard. He looked startled.

"Do you pretend you don't even know that?"

Carse reminded, "I told you I come from so far that this is all a new world to me."

Boghaz' fat face showed mixed incredulity and puzzlement. Finally he said, "I can't decide whether you're really what you say or whether you're pretending childish ignorance for your own reasons."

He shrugged. "Whichever is the case you could soon get the story from the others. I might as well be truthful."

He spoke in a rapid undertone, watching Carse shrewdly. "Even a remote barbarian will have heard of the superhuman Quiru, who long ago possessed all power and scientific wisdom. And of how the Cursed One among them, Rhiannon, sinned by teaching too much wisdom to the Dhuvians.

"Because of what that led to the Quiru left our world, going no man knows whither. But before they left they seized the sinner Rhiannon and locked him in a hidden tomb and locked in with him his instruments of awful power.

"Is it wonderful that all Mars has hunted that Tomb for an age? Is it strange that either the Empire of Sark or the Sea Kings would do anything to possess the Cursed One's lost powers? And now that you have found the Tomb, do I, Boghaz, blame you for being cautious with your secret?"

Carse ignored the last. He was remembering now—remembering those strange instruments of jewels and prisms and metal in Rhiannon's Tomb.

Were those really the secrets of an ancient, great science—a science that had long been lost to the half-barbaric Mars of this age?

He asked, "Who are these Sea Kings? I take it that they're enemies of the Sarks?"

Boghaz nodded. "Sark rules the lands east, north and south of the White Sea. But in the west are small free kingdoms of hardy sea-rovers like the Khonds and their Sea Kings defy the power of Sark."

He added, "Aye and there are many even in my own subject land of Valkis and elsewhere who secretly hate Sark because of the Dhuvians."

"The Dhuvians?" Carse repeated. "You mentioned them before. Who are they?"

Boghaz snorted. "Look, friend, it's all very well to pretend ignorance but that's carrying it too far! There's no tribesman from so far away that he doesn't know and fear the accursed Serpent!"

So the Serpent was a generic name from the mysterious Dhuvians? Why were they called so, Carse wondered?

Carse became suddenly aware that the woman Swimmer was looking at him fixedly. For a startled moment he had the eery sensation that she was looking into his thoughts.

"Shallah is watching us—best be quiet now," Boghaz whispered hastily. "Everyone knows that the Halflings can read the mind a little."

If that was so, Carse thought grimly, Shallah the Swimmer must have found profoundly astonishing matter in his own thoughts.

He had been pitchforked into a wholly unfamiliar Mars, most of which was still a mystery to him.

But if Boghaz spoke truth, if those strange objects in the Tomb of Rhiannon were instruments of a great lost scientific power, then even though he was a slave he held the key to a secret coveted by all this world.

That secret could be his death. He must guard it jealously till he won free of this brutal bondage. For a resolve to regain his freedom and a grim growing hatred of the swaggering Sarks were all that he was sure of now.

The sun rose high, blazing down into the unprotected oar pit. The wind that hummed through the taut cordage aloft did nothing to relieve the heat down here. The men broiled like fish on a griddle, and so far neither food nor water had been forthcoming.

Carse watched with sullen eyes the Sark soldiers lounging arrogantly on the deck above the sunken oar pit. On the after part of that deck rose the low main cabin, the door to which remained closed. Atop the flat roof stood the steersman, a husky Sark sailor who held the massive tiller and who took his orders from Scyld.

Scyld himself stood up there, his spade beard thrust up as he looked unseeingly over the misery in the oar pit toward the distant horizon. Occasionally he rapped out curt commands to the steersman.

Rations came at last—black bread and a pannikin of water, served out by one of the strange winged slaves Carse had glimpsed before in Jekkara. The Sky Folk, the mob had called them.

Carse studied this one with interest. He looked like a crippled angel, with his shining wings cruelly broken and his beautiful suffering face. He moved slowly along the catwalk at his task as though walking were a burden to him. He did not smile or speak and his eyes were veiled.

Shallah thanked him for her food. He did not look at her but went away, dragging his empty basket. She turned to Carse.

"Most of them," she said, "die when their wings are broken."

He knew she meant a death of the spirit. And sight of that broken-winged Halfling somehow gave Carse a bitterer hatred of the Sarks than his own enslavement had aroused. "Curse the brutes who would do a thing like that." he muttered.

"Aye, cursed be they who foregather in evil with the Serpent!" growled Jaxart, the big Khond at their oar. "Cursed be their king and his she-devil daughter Ywain! Had I the chance I'd sink us all beneath the waves to thwart whatever deviltry she's been hatching at Jekkara."

"Why hasn't she shown herself?" Carse asked. "Is she so delicate that she'll keep her cabin all the way to Sark?

"That hellcat delicate?" Jaxart spat in loathing and said, "She's wantoning with the lover hidden in her cabin. He crept aboard at Sark, all hooded and cloaked, and hasn't come out since. But we saw him."

Shallah looked aft with fixed gaze and murmured, "It is no lover she's hiding but accursed evil. I sensed it when it came aboard."

She turned her disturbing luminous gaze on Carse. "I think there is a curse on you too, stranger. I can feel it but cannot understand you."

Carse again felt a little chill. These Halflings with their extrasensory powers could just vaguely sense his incredible alienage. He was glad when Shallah and Naram, her mate, turned away from him.

Often in the hours that followed Carse found his gaze going up to the afterdeck. He had a grim desire to see this Ywain of Sark whose slave he now was.

In mid-afternoon, after blowing steadily for hours, the wind began to fail and dropped finally to a flat calm.

The drum thundered. The sweeps went out and once again Carse was sweating at the unfamiliar labor, snarling at the kiss of the lash on his back.

Only Boghaz seemed happy.

"I am no seafaring man," he said, shaking his head. "For a Khond like you, Jaxart, sea-roving is natural. But I was delicate in my youth and forced to quieter pursuits. Ah blessed calm! Even the drudgery of the oars is preferable to bounding like a wild thing over the waves."

Carse was touched by this pathetic speech until he discovered that Boghaz had good reason not to mind the rowing inasmuch as he was only bending back and forth while Carse and Jaxart pulled. Carse dealt him a blow that nearly knocked him off the bench and after that he pulled his weight, groaning.

The afternoon wore on, hot and endless, to the ceaseless beat of the oars.

The palms of Carse's hands blistered, then broke and bled. He was a powerful man, but even so the strength ran out of him like water and his body felt as though it had been stretched on the rack. He envied Jaxart, who behaved as though he had been born in the oar banks.

Gradually sheer exhaustion dulled his agony somewhat. He fell into a sort of drugged stupor, wherein his body performed its task mechanically.

Then, in the last golden blaze of daylight, he lifted his head to gasp for breath and saw, through the wavering haze that obscured his vision, a woman standing on the deck above him, looking at the sea.

CHAPTER SEVEN

The Sword

SHE MIGHT BE both Sark and devil as the others had said. But whatever she was, she stopped Carse's breath and held him staring.

She stood like a dark flame in a nimbus of sunset light. Her habit was that of a young warrior, a hauberk of black mail over a short purple tunic, with a jeweled dragon coiling on the curve of her mailed breast and a short sword at her side.

Her head was bare. She wore her black hair short, cut square above the eyes and falling to her shoulders. Under dark brows her eyes had smoldering fires in them. She stood with straight long legs braced slightly apart, peering out over the sea.

Carse felt the surge of a bitter admiration. This woman owned him and he hated her and all her race but he could not deny her burning beauty and her strength.

"*Row*, you carrion!"

The oath and the lash brought him back from his staring. He had lost stroke, fouling the whole starboard bank, and Jaxart was cursing and Callus was using the whip.

He beat them all impartially and fat Boghaz wailed at the top of his lungs, "Mercy, oh Lady Ywain! Mercy, mercy!"

"Shut up, scum!" snarled Callus and lashed them until blood ran.

Ywain glanced down into the pit. She rapped out a name. "Callus!"

The oar-bank captain bowed. "Yes, Highness."

"Pick up the beat," she said. "Faster, I want to raise the Black Banks at dawn." She looked directly at Carse and Boghaz and added, "Flog every man who loses stroke."

She turned away. The drum beat quickened. Carse looked with bitter eyes at Ywain's back. It would be good to tear her pride out by the roots and stamp on it.

The lash rapped out the time on his unwilling back and there was nothing for it but to row.

Jaxart grinned a wolf's grin. Between strokes he panted,

"Sark rules the White Sea to hear them tell it. But the Sea Kings still come out! Even Ywain won't dawdle on the way!"

"If their enemies may be out why don't they have escort ships for this galley?" Carse asked, gasping.

Jaxart shook his head. "That I can't understand myself. I heard that Garach sent his daughter to overawe the subject king of Jekkara, who's been getting too ambitious. But why she came without escort ships—"

Boghaz suggested, "Perhaps the Dhuvians furnished her with some of their mysterious weapons for protection?"

The big Khond snorted. "The Dhuvians are too crafty to do that! They'll use their strange weapons sometimes in behalf of their Sark allies, yes. That's why the alliance exists. But give weapons to Sark, teach Sarks how to use them? They're not *that* foolish!"

Carse was getting a clearer idea of this ancient Mars. These peoples were all half-barbaric—all but the mysterious Dhuvians. *They* apparently possessed at least some of the ancient science of this world and jealously guarded it and used it for their own and their Sark allies' purposes.

Night fell. Ywain remained on deck and the watches were doubled. Naram and Shallah, the two Swimmers, stirred restlessly in their shackles. In the torchlit gloom, their eyes were luminous with some secret excitement.

Carse had neither the strength nor the inclination to appreciate the wonder of the glowing sea by moonlight. To make matters worse, a headwind sprang up and roughened the waves to an ugly cross-chop that made the oars doubly difficult to handle. The drum beat inexorably.

A dull fury burned in Carse. He ached intolerably. He bled and his back was striped by fiery weals. The oar was heavy. It was heavier than all Mars and it bucked and fought him like a live thing.

Something happened to his face. A strange stony look came over it and all the color went out of his eyes, leaving them bleak as ice and not quite sane. The drumbeat merged into the pounding of his own heart, roaring louder with every painful stroke.

A wave sprang up, the long sweep crabbed, the handle took Carse across the chest and knocked the wind out of him. Jaxart, who was experienced, and Boghaz, who was heavy, regained control almost at once though not before the overseer was on hand to curse them for lazy carrion—his favorite word—and to lay on the whip.

Carse let go of the oar. He moved so fast, in spite of his hampering chains, that the overseer had no idea what was happening until suddenly he was lying across the Earthman's knees and trying to protect his head from the blows of the Earthman's wrist-cuffs.

Instantly the oar bank went mad. The stroke was hopelessly lost. Men shouted for the kill. Callus rushed up and hit Carse over the head with the loaded butt of his whip, knocking him half-senseless. The overseer scrambled back to safety, eluding Jaxart's clutching arms. Boghaz made himself as small as possible and did nothing.

Ywain's voice came down from the deck. "Callus!"

The oar-bank captain knelt, trembling, "Yes, Highness?"

"Flog them all until they remember that they're no longer men but slaves." Her angry, impersonal gaze rested on Carse. "As for that one—he's new, isn't he?"

"Yes, Highness."

"Teach him," she said.

They taught him. Callus and the overseer together taught him. Carse bowed his head over his arms and took it. Now and again Boghaz screamed as the lash flicked too far over and caught him instead. Between his feet Carse saw dimly the red streams that trickled down into the bilges and stained the water. The rage that had burned in him chilled and altered as iron tempers under the hammer.

At last they stopped. Carse raised his head. It was the greatest effort he had ever made, but stiffly, stubbornly, he raised it. He looked directly at Ywain.

"Have you learned your lesson, slave?" she asked.

It was a long time before he could form the words to answer. He was beyond caring now whether he lived or died. His whole universe was centered on the woman who stood arrogant and untouchable above him.

"Come down yourself and teach me if you can," he answered hoarsely and called her a name in the lowest vernacular of the streets—a name that said there was nothing she could teach a man.

For a moment no one moved or spoke. Carse saw her face go white and he laughed, a hoarse terrible sound in the silence. Then Scyld drew his sword and vaulted over the rail into the oar pit.

The blade flashed high and bright in the torchlight. It occurred to Carse that he had traveled a long way to die. He waited for the stroke but it did not come and then he realized that Ywain had cried out to Scyld to stop.

Scyld faltered, then turned, puzzled, looking up. "But Highness—"

"Come here," she said, and Carse saw that she was staring at the sword in Scyld's hand, the sword of Rhiannon.

Scyld climbed the ladder back up to the deck, his black-browed face a little frightened. Ywain met him.

"Give me that," she said. And when he hesitated, "The sword, fool!"

He laid it in her hands and she stood looking at it, turning it over in the torchlight, studying the workmanship, the hilt with its single smoky jewel, the etched symbols on the blade.

"Where did you get this, Scyld?"

"I—" he stammered, not liking to make the admission, his hand going instinctively to his stolen collar.

Ywain snapped, "Your thieving doesn't interest me. Where did you get it?"

He pointed to Carse and Boghaz. "From them, Highness, when I picked them up."

She nodded. "Fetch them aft to my quarters."

She disappeared inside the cabin. Scyld, unhappy and completely bewildered, turned to obey her order, and Boghaz moaned.

"Oh, merciful gods!" he whispered. "That's done it!" He leaned closer to Carse and said rapidly while he still had the chance, "Lie, as you never lied before! If she thinks you know the secret of the Tomb she or the Dhuvians will force it out of you!"

Carse said nothing. He was having all he could do to retain consciousness. Scyld called profanely for wine, which was brought. He forced some of it down Carse's throat, then had him and Boghaz released from the oar and marched up to the afterdeck.

The wine and the sea wind up on deck revived Carse enough so that he could keep his feet under him. Scyld ushered them ungently into Ywain's torchlit cabin, where she sat with the sword of Rhiannon laid on the carven table before her.

In the opposite bulkhead was a low door leading into an inner cabin. Carse saw that it was open the merest crack. No light showed but he got the feeling that someone—something—was crouching behind it, listening. It made him remember Jaxart's word and Shallah's.

There was a taint in the air—a faint musky odor, dry and sickly. It seemed to come from that inner cabin. It had a strange effect on Carse. Without knowing what it was he hated it.

He thought that if it was a lover Ywain was hiding in there it must be a strange sort of lover. Ywain took his mind off that. Her gaze stabbed at him, and once again he thought that he had never seen such eyes. Then she said to Scyld, "Tell me—the full story."

Uncomfortably, in halting sentences, he told her. Ywain looked at Boghaz.

"And you, fat one. How did you come by the sword?"

Boghaz sighed, nodded at Carse. "From him, Highness. It's a handsome weapon and I'm a thief by trade."

"Is that the only reason you wanted it?"

Boghaz' face was a model of innocent surprise. "What other reason could there be? I'm no fighting man. Besides, there were the belt and collar. You can see for yourself, Highness, that all are valuable."

Her face did not show whether she believed him or not. She turned to Carse.

"The sword belonged to you, then?"

"Yes."

"Where did you get it?"

"I bought it from a trader."

"Where?"

"In the northern country, beyond Shun."

Ywain smiled. "You lie."

Carse said wearily, "I came by the weapon honestly"—he had, in a sense—"and I don't care whether you believe it or not."

The crack of that inner door mocked Carse. He wanted to break it open, to see what crouched there, listening, watching out of the darkness. He wanted to see what made that hateful smell.

Almost, it seemed, there was no need for that. Almost, it seemed, he knew.

Unable to contain himself any longer, Scyld burst out, "Your pardon, Highness! But why all this fuss about a sword?"

"You're a good soldier, Scyld," she answered thoughtfully, "but in many ways a blockhead. Did you clean this blade?"

"Of course. And bad condition it was in, too." He glanced disgustedly at Carse. "It looked as though he hadn't touched it for years."

Ywain reached out and laid her hand upon the jeweled hilt. Carse saw that it trembled. She said softly, "You were right, Scyld. It hadn't been touched, for years. Not since Rhiannon, who made it, was walled away in his tomb to suffer for his sins."

Scyld's face went completely blank. His jaw dropped. After a long while he said one word, "Rhiannon!"

CHAPTER EIGHT

The Thing in the Dark

YWAIN'S LEVEL GAZE fastened on Carse. "He knows the secret of the Tomb, Scyld. He must know it if he had the sword."

She paused and when she spoke again her words were almost inaudible, like the voicing of an inner thought.

"A dangerous secret. So dangerous that I almost wish . . ."

She broke off short, as though she had already said too much. Did she glance quickly at the inner door?

In her old imperious tone she said to Carse, "One more chance, slave. Where is the Tomb of Rhiannon?"

Carse shook his head. "I know nothing," he said and gripped Boghaz' shoulder to steady himself. Little crimson droplets had trickled down to dye the rug under his feet. Ywain's face seemed far away.

Scyld said hoarsely, "Give him to me, Highness."

"No. He's too far gone for your methods now. I don't want him killed yet. I must—take thought to this."

She frowned, looking from Carse to Boghaz and back again.

"They object to rowing, I believe. Very well. Take the third man off their oar. Let these two work it without help all night. And tell Callus to lay the lash on the fat one twice in every glass, five strokes."

Boghaz wailed. "Highness, I implore you! I would tell if I could but I know nothing. I swear it!"

She shrugged. "Perhaps not. In that case you will wish to persuade your comrade to talk."

She turned again to Scyld. "Tell Callus also to douse the tall one with sea water, as often as he needs it." Her white teeth glinted. "It has a healing property."

Scyld laughed.

Ywain motioned to him to go. "See that they're kept at it but on no account is either one to die. When they're ready to talk bring them to me."

Scyld saluted and marched his prisoners back again to the rowers' pit. Jaxart was taken off the oar and the endless nightmare of the dark hours continued for Carse.

Boghaz was crushed and trembling. He screamed mightily as he took his five strokes and then moaned in Carse's ear, "I wish I'd never seen your bloody sword! She'll take us to Caer Dhu—and the gods have mercy on us."

Carse bared his teeth in what might have been a grin. "You talked differently in Jekkara."

"I was a free man then and the Dhuvians were far away."

Carse felt some deep and buried nerve contract at the mention of that name. He said in an odd voice, "Boghaz, what was that smell in the cabin?"

"Smell? I noticed none."

"Strange," Carse thought, *"when it drove me nearly mad. Or perhaps I'm mad already."*

"Jaxart was right, Boghaz. There is something hidden there, in the inner cabin."

With some irritation Boghaz said, "Ywain's wantoning is nothing to me."

They labored in silence for a while. Then Carse asked abruptly, "Who are the Dhuvians?"

Boghaz stared at him. "Where do you really come from, man?"

"As I told you—from far beyond Shun."

"It must have been from far indeed if you haven't heard of Caer Dhu and the Serpent!"

Then Boghaz shrugged fat shoulders as he labored. "You're playing some deep game of your own, I suppose. All this pretended ignorance—but I don't mind playing that game with you."

He went on, "You know at least that since long ago there have been human peoples on our world and also the not-quite-human peoples, the Halflings. Of the humans the great Quiru, who are gone, were the greatest. They had so much science and wisdom that they're still revered as superhuman.

"But there were also the Halflings—the races who are man-like but not descended of the same blood. The Swimmers, who sprang from the sea-creatures, and the Sky Folk, who came from the winged things—and the Dhuvians, who are from the serpent."

A cold breath swept through Carse. Why was it that all this which he heard for the first time seemed so familiar to him?

Certainly he had never heard before this story of ancient Martian evolution, of intrinsically alien stocks evolving into su-perficially similar pseudo human peoples. He had not heard it before—*or had he?*

"Crafty and wise as the snake that fathered them were the Dhuvians always," Boghaz was continuing. "So crafty that they prevailed on Rhiannon of the Quiru to teach them some of his science.

"Some but not all! Yet what they learned was enough that they could make their black city of Caer Dhu impregnable and could occasionally intervene with their scientific weapons so as to make their Sark allies the dominant human nation."

"And *that* was Rhiannon's sin?" Carse said.

"Aye, that was the Cursed One's sin for in his pride he had defied the other Quiru, who counseled him not to teach the Dhuvians such powers. For that sin the other Quiru condemned Rhiannon and entombed him in a hidden place before they left our world. At least so says the legend."

"But the Dhuvians themselves are no mere legend?"

"They are not, damn them," Boghaz muttered. "They are the reason all free men hate the Sarks, who hold evil alliance with the Serpent."

They were interrupted by the broken-winged slave, Lorn. He had been sent to dip up a bucket of sea water and now appeared with it.

The winged man spoke and now his voice had music in it. "This will be painful, stranger. Bear it if you can—it will help you." He raised the bucket. Glowing water spilled out, covering Carse's body with a bright sheath.

Carse knew why Ywain had smiled. Whatever chemical gave the sea its phosphorescence might be healing but the cure was worse than the wounds. The corrosive agony seemed to eat the flesh from his bones.

The night wore on and after a while Carse felt the pain grow less. His weals no longer bled and the water began to refresh him. To his own surprise he saw the second dawn break over the White Sea.

Soon after sunrise a cry came down from the masthead. The Black Banks lay ahead.

Through the oar port Carse saw a welter of broken water that stretched for miles. Reefs and shoals, with here and there black jagged fangs of rock showing through the foam. "They're not going to try to run that mess?" he exclaimed.

"It's the shortest route to Sark," Boghaz said. "As for running the Banks—why do you suppose every Sark galley carries captive Swimmers?"

"I've wondered."

"You'll soon see."

Ywain came on deck and Scyld joined her. They did not look down at the two haggard scarecrows sweating at the oar.

Boghaz instantly wailed piteously. "Mercy, Highness!"

Ywain paid no attention. She ordered Scyld, "Slow the beat and send the Swimmers out."

Naram and Shallah were unshackled and ran forward. Metal harnesses were locked to their bodies. Long wire lines ran from these harnesses to ringbolts in the forecastle deck.

The two Swimmers dived fearlessly into the foaming waters. The wire lines tautened and Carse glimpsed the heads of the two bobbing like corks as they swam smoothly ahead of the galley into the roaring Banks.

"You see?" said Boghaz. "They feel out the channel. They can guide a ship through anything."

To the slow beat of the drum the black galley forged into the broken water.

Ywain stood, hair flying in the breeze and hauberk shining, by the man at the tiller. She and Scyld peered closely ahead. The rough waters shook along the keel with a hiss and a snarl and once an oar splintered on a rock but they crept on safely.

It was a long slow weary passage. The sun rose toward the zenith. There was an aching tension aboard the galley.

Carse only dimly heard the roar of breakers as he and Boghaz labored at their oar. The fat Valkisian was groaning ceaselessly now. Carse's arms felt like lead, his brain seemed clamped in steel.

At last, the galley found smooth water, shot clear of the Banks. Their dull thunder came now from astern. The Swimmers were hauled back in.

Ywain glanced down into the oar pit for the first time, at the staggering slaves.

"Give them a brief rest," she replied. "The wind should rise soon."

Her eyes swung to Carse and Boghaz. "And, Scyld, I'll see those two again now."

Carse watched Scyld cross the deck and come down the ladder. He felt a sick apprehension.

He did not want to go up to that cabin again. He did not want to see again that door with its mocking crack nor smell that sickly evil smell.

But he and Boghaz were again unshackled and herded aft, and there was nothing he could do.

The door swung shut behind them. Scyld, Ywain behind the carved table, the sword of Rhiannon gleaming before her. The tainted air and the low door of the bulkhead, not quite closed—not quite.

Ywain spoke. "You've had the first taste of what I can do to you. Do you want the second? Or will you tell me the location of Rhiannon's Tomb and what you found there?"

Carse answered tonelessly. "I told you before that I don't know."

He was not looking at Ywain. That inner door fascinated him, held his gaze. Somewhere, far at the back of his mind, something stirred and woke. A prescience, a hate, a horror that he could not understand.

But he understood well enough that this was the climax, the end. A deep shudder ran through him, an involuntary tightening of nerves.

"What is it that I do not know but can somehow almost remember?"

Ywain leaned forward. "You're strong. You pride yourself on that. You feel that you can stand physical punishment, perhaps more than I would dare to give you. I think you could. But there are other ways. Quicker, surer ways and even a strong man has no defense against them."

She followed the line of his gaze to the inner door. "Perhaps," she said softly, "you can guess what I mean."

Carse's face was empty now of all expression. The musky smell was heavy as smoke in his throat. He felt it coil and writhe inside him, filling his lungs, stealing into his blood. Poisonously subtle, cruel, cold with a primal coldness. He swayed on his feet but his fixed stare did not waver.

He said hoarsely, "I can guess."

"Good. Speak now and that door need not open."

Carse laughed, a low, harsh sound. His eyes were clouded and strange.

"Why should I speak? You would only destroy me later to keep the secret safe."

He stepped forward. He knew that he moved. He knew that he spoke though the sound of his own voice was vague in his ears.

But there was a dark confusion in him. The veins of his temples stood out like knotted cords, and the blood throbbed in his brain. Pressure as of something bursting, breaking its bonds, tearing itself free.

He did not know why he stepped forward, toward that door. He did not know why he cried out in a tone that was not his, *"Open then, Child of the Snake!"*

Boghaz let out a wailing shriek and crouched down in a corner, hiding his face. Ywain started up, astonished and suddenly pale. The door swung slowly back.

There was nothing behind it but darkness and a shadow. A shadow cloaked and hooded and so crouched in the lightless cabin that it was no more than the ghost of a shadow.

But it was there. And the man Carse, caught fast in the trap of his strange fate, recognized it for what it was.

It was fear, the ancient evil thing that crept among the grasses in the beginning, apart from life but watching it with eyes of cold wisdom, laughing its silent laughter, giving nothing but the bitter death.

It was the Serpent.

The primal ape in Carse wanted to run, to hide away. Every cell of his flesh recoiled, every instinct warned him.

But he did not run and there was an anger in him that grew until it blotted out fear, blotted out Ywain and the others, everything but the wish to destroy utterly the creature crouching beyond the light.

His own anger—or something greater? Something born of a shame and an agony that he could never know?

A voice spoke to him out of the darkness, soft and sibilant.

"You have willed it. Let it be so."

There was utter silence in the cabin. Scyld had recoiled. Even Ywain had drawn back to the end of the table. The cowering Boghaz hardly breathed.

The shadow had stirred with a slight, dry rustle. A spot of subdued brilliance had appeared, held by unseen hands—a brilliance that shed no glow around it. It seemed to Carse like a ring of little stars, incredibly distant.

The stars began to move, to circle their hidden orbit, to spin faster and faster until they became a wheel, peculiarly blurred. From them now came a thin high note, a crystal song that was like infinity, without beginning and end.

A song, a call attuned to his hearing alone? Or was it his hearing? He could not tell. Perhaps he heard it with his flesh instead, with every grieving nerve. The others, Ywain and Scyld and Boghaz, seemed unaffected.

Carse felt a coldness stealing over him. It was as though those tiny singing stars called to him across the universe, charming him out into the deeps of space where the empty cosmos sucked him dry of warmth and life.

His muscles loosened. He felt his sinews melt and flow away on the icy tide. He felt his brain dissolving.

He went slowly to his knees. The little stars sang on and on. He understood them now. They were asking him a question. He knew that when he answered he could sleep. He would not awake again but that did not matter. He was afraid now but if he slept he would forget his fear.

Fear—fear! The old, old racial terror that haunts the soul, the dread that slides in the quite dark—

In sleep and death he could forget that fear. He need only answer that hypnotic whispered question.

"Where is the Tomb?"

Answer. Speak. But something still chained his tongue. The red flame of anger still flickered in him, fighting the brilliance of the singing stars.

He struggled but the star-song was too strong. He heard his dry lips slowly speaking. "The Tomb, the place of Rhiannon . . ."

"Rhiannon! Dark Father who taught you power, thou spawn of the serpent's egg!"

The name rang in him like a battle cry. His rage soared up. The smoky jewel in the hilt of the sword on the table seemed suddenly to call to his hand. He leaped and grasped its hilt.

Ywain sprang forward with a startled cry but was too late.

The great jewel seemed to blaze, to catch up the power of the singing, shining stars and hurl it back.

The crystal song keened and broke. The brilliance faded. He had shattered the strange hypnosis.

Blood flowed again into Carse's veins. The sword felt alive in his hands. He shouted the name Rhiannon and plunged forward into the dark.

He heard a hissing scream as his long blade went home to the heart of the shadow.

CHAPTER NINE
Galley of Death

CARSE STRAIGHTENED SLOWLY and turned in the doorway, his back to the thing he had slain but had not seen. He had no wish to see it. He was utterly shaken and in a strange mood, full of a vaulting strength that verged on madness.

The hysteria, he thought, that comes when you've taken too much, when the walls close in and there's nothing to do but fight before you die.

The cabin was full of a stunned silence. Scyld had the staring look of an idiot, his mouth fallen open. Ywain had put one hand to the edge of the table and it was strange to see in her that one small sign of weakness. She had not taken her eyes from Carse.

She said huskily. "Are you man or demon that you can stand against Caer Dhu?"

Carse did not answer. He was beyond speech. Her face floated before him like a silver mask. He remembered the pain, the shameful labor at the sweep, the scars of the lash that he carried. He remembered the voice that had said to Callus, "Teach him!"

He had slain the Serpent. After that it seemed an easy thing to kill a queen.

He began to move, covering the few short steps that lay between them, and there was something terrible about the slow purposefulness of it, the galled and shackled slave carrying the great sword, its blade dark with alien blood.

Ywain gave back one step. Her hand faltered to her own hilt. She was not afraid of death. She was afraid of the thing that she saw in Carse, the light that blazed in his eyes. A fear of the soul and not the body.

Scyld gave a hoarse cry. He drew his sword and lunged.

They had all forgotten Boghaz, crouching quiet in his corner. Now the Valkisian rose to his feet, handling his great bulk with unbelievable speed. As Scyld passed him he raised both hands and brought the full weight of his gyves down with tremendous strength on the Sark's head.

Scyld dropped like a stone.

And now Ywain had found her pride again. The sword of Rhiannon rose high for the death stroke and quick, quick as lightning, she drew her own short blade and parried it as it fell.

The force of the blow drove her weapon out of her hands. Carse had only to strike again. But it seemed that with that effort something had gone out of him. He saw her mouth open to voice an angry shout for aid and he struck her across the face with his hilt reversed, so that she slid stunned to the deck, her cheek laid open.

And then Boghaz was thrusting him back, saying, "Don't kill her! We may buy our lives with hers!"

Carse watched as Boghaz bound and gagged her and took the dagger from her belt sheath.

It occurred to him that they were two slaves who had overpowered Ywain of Sark and struck down her captain and that the lives of Matt Carse and Boghaz of Valkis were worth less than a puff of wind as soon as it was discovered.

So far, they were safe. There had been little noise and there were no sounds of alarm outside.

Boghaz shut the inner door as though to block off even the memory of what lay within. Then he took a closer look at Scyld, who was quite dead. He picked up the man's sword and stood still for a minute, catching his breath.

He was staring at Carse with a new respect that had in it both awe and fear. Glancing at the closed door, he muttered, "I would not have believed it possible. And yet I saw it." He turned back to Carse. "You cried out upon Rhiannon before you struck. Why?"

Carse said impatiently, "How can a man know what he's saying, at a time like that?"

The truth was that he didn't know himself why he had spoken the Cursed One's name, except that it had been thrust at him so often that he supposed it had become a sort of obsession. The Dhuvian's little hypnosis gadget had thrown his whole mind off balance for a while. He remembered only a towering rage—the gods knew he had had enough to make any many angry.

It was probably not so strange that the Dhuvian's hypnotic science hadn't been able to put him completely under. After all he was an Earthman and a product of another age. Even so it had been a near thing—horribly near. He didn't want to think about it any more.

"That's over now. Forget it. We've got to think how to get ourselves out of this mess."

Boghaz' courage seemed to have drained away. He said glumly, "We'd better kill ourselves at once and have done with it."

He meant it. Carse said, "If you feel that way why did you strike out to save my life?"

"I don't know. Instinct, I suppose."

"All right. My instinct is to go on living as long as possible."

It didn't look as though that would be very long. But he was not going to take Boghaz' advice and fall upon the sword of Rhiannon. He weighted it in his hands, scowling, and then looked from it to his fetters.

He said suddenly, "If we could free the rowers they'd fight. They're all condemned for life—nothing to lose. We might take the ship."

Boghaz' eyes widened, then narrowed shrewdly. He thought it over. Then he shrugged. "I suppose one can always die. It's worth trying. Anything's worth trying."

He tested the point of Ywain's dagger. It was thin and strong. With infinite skill, he began to pick the lock of the Earthman's gyves.

"Have you a plan?" he asked.

Carse grunted. "I'm no magician. I can only try." He glanced at Ywain. "You stay here, Boghaz. Barricade the door. Guard her. If things go wrong she's our last and only hope."

The cuffs hung loose now on his wrist and ankles. Reluctantly he laid down the sword. Boghaz would need the dagger to free himself but there was another one on Scyld's body. Carse took it and hid it under his kilt. As he did so he gave Boghaz a few brief instructions.

A moment later Carse opened the cabin door just widely enough to step outside. From behind him came a good enough imitation of Scyld's gruff voice, calling for a guard. A soldier came.

"Take this slave back to the oar bank," ordered the voice that aped Scyld's. "And see that the lady Ywain is not disturbed."

The man saluted and began to herd the shuffling Carse away. The cabin door banged shut and Carse heard the sound of the bar dropping into place.

Across the deck, and down the ladder. *"Count the soldiers, think how it must be done!"*

No. Don't think. Don't, or you'll never try it.

The drummer, who was a slave himself. The two Swimmers. The overseer, up at the forward end of the catwalk, lashing a rower. Rows of shoulders, bending over the oars, back and forth. Rows of faces above them. The faces of rats, of jackals, of wolves. The creak and groan of the looms, the reek of sweat and bilge water, the incessant beat, beat, beat of the drum.

The soldier turned Carse over to Callus and went away. Jaxart was back on the oar and with him a lean Sark convict with a brand on his face. They glanced up at Carse and then away again.

Callus thrust the Earthman roughly onto the bench, where he bent low over the oar. Callus stooped to fix the master chain to his leg irons, growling as he did so.

"I hope that Ywain lets me have you when she's all through with you, carrion! I'll have fun while you last—"

Callus stopped very suddenly and said no more, then or ever. Carse had stabbed his heart with such swift neatness that not even Callus was aware of the stroke until he ceased to breathe.

"Keep stroke!" snarled Carse to Jaxart under his breath. The big Khond obeyed. A smoldering light came into his eyes. The branded man laughed once, silently, with a terrible eagerness.

Carse cut the key to the master locks free from its thong on Callus' girdle and let the corpse down gently into the bilges.

The man across the catwalk on the port oar had seen as had the drummer. "Keep stroke!" said Carse again and Jaxart glared and the stroke was kept. But the drum beat faltered and died.

Carse shook off his manacles. His eyes met the drummer's and the rhythm started again but already the overseer was on his way aft, shouting.

"What's the matter there, you pig?"

"My arms are weary," the man quavered.

"Weary, are they? I'll weary your back for you too if it happens again!"

The man on the port oar, a Khond, said deliberately. "Much is going to happen, you Sark scum." He took his hands off the oar.

The overseer advanced upon him. "Is it now? Why, the filth is a very prophet!"

His lash rose and fell once and then Carse was on him. One hand clamped the man's mouth shut and the other plunged the dagger in. Swiftly, silently, a second body rolled into the bilges.

A deep animal cry broke out along the oar bank and was choked down as Carse raised his arms in a warning gesture, looking upward at the deck. No one had noticed yet. There had been nothing to draw notice.

Inevitably, the rhythm of the oars had broken but that was not unusual and, in any case, it was the concern of the overseer. Unless it stopped altogether no one would wonder. If luck would only hold . . .

The drummer had the sense or the habit to keep on. Carse passed the word along—"Keep stroke, until we're all free!" The beat picked up again, slowly. Crouching low, Carse opened the master locks. The men needed no warning to be easy with their chains as they freed themselves, one by one.

Even so, less than half of them were loose when an idle soldier chose to lean on the deck rail and look down.

Carse had just finished releasing the Swimmers. He saw the man's expression change from boredom to incredulous awareness and he caught up the overseer's whip and sent the long lash singing upward. The soldier bellowed the alarm as the lash coiled around his neck and brought him crashing down into the pit.

Carse leaped to the ladder. "Come on, you scum, you rabble!" he shouted. "Here's your chance!"

And they were after him like one man, roaring the beast roar of creatures hungry for vengeance and blood. Up the ladder they poured, swinging their chains, and those that were still held to the benches worked like madmen to be free.

They had the brief advantage of surprise, for the attack had come so quickly on the heels of the alarm that swords were still half drawn, bows still unstrung. But it wouldn't last long. Carse knew well how short a time it would last.

"Strike! Strike hard while you can!"

With belaying pins, with their shackles, and with their fists, the galley slaves charged in and the soldiers met them. Carse with his whip and his knife, Jaxart howling the word *Khondor* like a battle-cry, naked bodies against mail, desperation against discipline. The Swimmers slipped like brown shadows through the fray and the slave with the broken wings had somehow possessed himself of a sword. Seamen reinforced the soldiers but still the wolves came up out the pit.

From the forecastle and the steersman's platform bowmen began to take their toll but the fight became so closely locked that they had to stop for fear of killing their own men. The salt-sweet smell of blood rose on the air. The decks were slippery with it. And gradually the superior force of the soldiery began to tell. Carse saw that the slaves were being driven back and the number of the dead was growing.

In a furious surge he broke through to the cabin. The Sarks must have thought it strange that Ywain and Scyld had not appeared but they had had little time to do anything about it. Carse pounded on the cabin door, shouting Boghaz' name.

The Valkisian drew the bar, and Carse burst in.

"Carry the wench up to the steersman's platform," he panted. "I'll cut your way."

He snatched up the sword of Rhiannon and went out again with Boghaz behind him, bearing Ywain in his arms.

The ladder was only a short two paces from the door. The bowmen had come down to fight and there was no one up on the platform but the frightened Sark sailor who clung to the tiller bar. Carse, swinging the great sword, cleared the way and held the ladder foot while Boghaz climbed up and set Ywain on her feet where all could see her.

"Look you!" he bellowed. "We have Ywain!"

He did not need to tell them. The sight of her, bound and gagged in the hands of a slave, was like a blow to the soldiers and like a magic potion to the rebels. Two mingled sounds went up, a groan and a cheer.

Someone found Scyld's body and dragged it out on deck. Doubly leaderless now, the Sarks lost heart. The tide of battle turned then and the slaves took their advantages in both hands.

The sword of Rhiannon led them. It slashed the halliards that brought the dragon flag of Sark plunging down from the masthead. And under its blade the last Sark soldier died.

There was an abrupt cessation of sound and movement. The black galley drifted with the freshening wind. The sun was low on the horizon. Carse climbed wearily to the steersman's platform.

Ywain, still fast in Boghaz's grip, followed him, eyes full of hellfire.

Carse went to the forward edge of the platform and stood leaning on the sword. The slaves, exhausted with fighting and drunk with victory, gathered on the deck below like a ring of panting wolves.

Jaxart came out from searching the cabins. He shook his dripping blade up at Ywain and shouted, "A fine lover she kept in her cabin! The spawn of Caer Dhu, the stinking Serpent!"

There was an instant reaction from the slaves. They were tense and bristling again at that name, afraid even in their numbers. Carse made his voice heard with difficulty.

"The thing is dead. Jaxart—will you cleanse the ship?"

Jaxart paused before he turned to obey. "How did you know it is dead?"

Carse said, "I killed it."

The men stared up at him as though he were something more than human. The awed muttering went around—"He slew the Serpent!"

With another man Jaxart returned to the cabin and brought the body out. No word was spoken. A wide lane was cleared to the lee rail and the black, shrouded thing was carried along it, faceless, formless, hidden in its robe and cowl, symbol even in death of infinite evil.

Again Carse fought down that cold repellent fear and the touch of strange anger. He forced himself to watch.

The splash it made as it fell was shockingly loud in the stillness. Ripples spread in little lines of fire and died away.

Then men began to talk again. They began to shout up to Ywain, taunting her. Someone yelled for her blood and there would have been a stampede up the ladder but that Carse threated them with his long blade.

"No! She's our hostage and worth her weight in gold."

He did not specify how but he knew the argument would satisfy them for a while. And much as he hated Ywain he somehow did not want to see her torn to pieces by this pack of wild beasts.

He steered their thoughts to another subject.

"We have to have a leader now. Whom will you choose?"

There was only one answer to that. They roared his name until it deafened him, and Carse felt a savage pleasure at he sound of it. After days of torment it was good to know he was a man again, even in an alien world.

When he could make himself heard he said, "All right. Now listen well. The Sarks will kill us by slow death for what we've done—*if* they catch us. So here's my plan. We'll join the free rovers, the Sea Kings who lair at Kondor!"

To the last man they agreed and the name *Khondor* rang up into the sunset sky.

The Khonds among the slaves were like wild men. One of them stripped a length of yellow cloth from the tunic of a dead soldier, fashioned a banner out of it and ran it up in place of the dragon flag of Sark.

At Carse's request, Jaxart took over the handling of the galley and Boghaz carried Ywain down again and locked her in the cabin.

The men dispersed, eager to be rid of their shackles, eager to loot the bodies of clothes and weapons and to dip into the wine casks. Only Naram and Shallah remained, looking up at Carse in the afterglow.

"Do you disagree?" he asked them.

Shallah's eyes glowed with the same eery light that he had seen in them before.

"You are a stranger," she said softly. "Stranger to us, stranger to our world. And I say again that I can sense a black shadow in you that makes me afraid, for you will cast it wherever you go."

She turned from him then and Naram said, "We go homeward now."

The two Swimmers poised for a moment on the rail. They were free now, free of their chains, and their bodies ached with the joy of it, stretching upward, supple, sure. Then they vanished overside.

After a moment Carse saw them again, rolling and plunging like dolphins, racing each other, calling to each other in their soft clear voices as they made the waves foam flame.

Deimos was already high. The afterglow was gone and Phobos came up swiftly out of the east. The sea turned glowing silver. The Swimmers went away toward the west, trailing their wakes of fire, a tracery of sparkling light that grew fainter and vanished altogether.

The black galley stood on for Khondor, her taut sails dark against the sky. And Carse remained as he was, standing on the platform, holding the sword of Rhiannon between his hands.

CHAPTER TEN
The Sea Kings

CARSE WAS LEANING on the rail, watching the sea, when the Sky Folk came. Time and distance had dropped behind the galley. Carse had rested. He wore a clean kilt, he was washed and shaven, his wounds were healing. He had regained his ornaments and the hilt of the long sword gleamed above his left shoulder.

Boghaz was beside him. Boghaz was always beside him. He pointed now to the western sky and said, "Look there."

Carse saw what he took to be a flight of birds in the distance. But they grew rapidly larger and presently he realized that they were men, or half-men, like the slave with the broken wings.

They were not slaves and their wings stretched wide, flashing in the sun. Their slim bodies, completely naked, gleamed like ivory. They were incredibly beautiful, arrowing down out of the blue.

They had a kinship with the Swimmers. The Swimmers were the perfect children of the sea and these were brother to wind and cloud and the clean immensity of the sky. It was as though some master hand had shaped them both out of separate elements, moulding them in strength and grace that was freed from all the earth-bound clumsiness of men, dreams made into joyous flesh.

Jaxart, who was at the helm, called down to them, "Scouts from Khondor!"

Carse mounted to the platform. The men gathered on the deck to watch as the four Sky Folk came down in a soaring rush.

Carse glanced forward to the sheer of the prow. Lorn, the winged slave, had taken to brooding there by himself, speaking to no one. Now he stood erect and one of the four went to him.

The others came to rest on the platform, folding their bright wings with a whispering rustle.

They greeted Jaxart by name, looking curiously at the long black galley and the hard-bitten mongrel crew that sailed her and, above all, at Carse. There was something in their searching gaze that reminded the Earthman uncomfortably of Shallah.

"Our chief," Jaxart told them. "A barbarian from the back door of Mars but a man of his hands and no fool, either. The Swimmers will have told the tale, how he took the ship and Ywain of Sark together."

"Aye." They acknowledged Carse with grave courtesy.

The Earthman said, "Jaxart has told me that all who fight Sark may have freedom of Khondor. I claim that right."

"We will carry word to Rold, who heads the council of the Sea Kings."

The Khonds on deck began to shout their own messages then, the eager words of men who have been a long time away from home. The Sky Men answered in their clear sweet voices and presently darted away, their pinions beating up into the blue air, higher and higher, growing tiny in the distance.

Lorn remained standing in the bow, watching until there was nothing left but empty sky.

"We'll raise Khondor soon," said Jaxart and Carse turned to speak to him. Then some instinct made him look back, and he saw that Lorn was gone.

There was no sign of him in the water. He had gone overside without a sound and he must have sunk like a drowning bird, pulled down by the weight of his useless wings.

Jaxart growled, "It was his will and better so." He cursed the Sarks and Carse smiled an ugly smile.

"Take heart," he said, "we may thrash them yet. How is it that Khondor has held out when Jekkara and Valkis fell?"

"Because not even the scientific weapons of the Sarks' evil allies, the Dhuvians, can touch us there. You'll understand why when you see Khondor."

Before noon they sighted land, a rocky and forbidding coast. The cliffs rose sheer out of the sea and behind them forested mountains towered like a giant's wall. Here and there a narrow fiord sheltered a fishing village and an occasional lonely steading clung to the high pasture land, a collar of white flame along the cliffs.

Carse sent Boghaz to the cabin for Ywain. She had remained there under guard and he had not seen her since the mutiny—except once.

It had been the first night after the mutiny. He had with Boghaz and Jaxart been examining the strange instruments that they had found in the inner cabin of the Dhuvian.

"These are Dhuvian weapons that only they know how to use," Boghaz had declared. "Now we know why Ywain had no escort ship. She needed none with a Dhuvian and his weapons aboard her galley."

Jaxart looked at the things with loathing and fear. "Science of the accursed Serpent! We should throw them after his body."

"No," Carse said, examining the things. "If it were possible to discover the way in which these devices operate—"

He had soon found that it would not be possible without prolonged study. He knew science fairly well, yes. But it was the science of his own different world.

These instruments had been built out of a scientific knowledge alien in nearly every way to his own. The science of Rhiannon, of which these Dhuvian weapons represented but a small part!

Carse could recognize the little hypnosis machine that the Dhuvian had used upon him in the dark. A little metal wheel set with crystal stars, that revolved by a slight pressure of the fingers. And when he set it turning it whispered a singing note that so chilled his blood with memory that he hastily set the thing down.

The other Dhuvian instruments were even more incomprehensible. One consisted of a large lens surrounded by oddly asymmetrical crystal prisms. Another had a heavy metal base in which flat metal vibrations were mounted. He could only guess that these weapons exploited the laws of alien and subtle optical and sonic sciences.

"No man can understand the Dhuvian science," muttered Jaxart. "Not even the Sarks, who have alliance with the Serpent."

He stared at the instruments with the half-superstitious hatred of a nonscientific folk for mechanical weapons.

"But perhaps Ywain, who is daughter of Sark's king, might know," Carse speculated. "It's worth trying."

He went to the cabin where she was being guarded with that purpose in mind. Ywain sat there and she wore now the shackles he had worn.

He came in upon her suddenly, catching her as she sat with her head bowed and her shoulders bent in utter weariness. But at the sound of the door she straightened and watched him, level-eyed. He saw how white her face was and how the shadows lay in the hollows of the bones.

He did not speak for a long time. He had no pity for her. He looked at her, liking the taste of victory, liking the thought that he could do what he wanted with her.

When he asked her about the Dhuvian scientific weapons they had found Ywain laughed mirthlessly.

"You must be an ignorant barbarian indeed if you think the Dhuvians would instruct even me in their science. One of them came with me to overawe with those things the Jekkaran ruler, who was waxing rebellious. But S'San would not let me even touch those things."

Carse believed her. It accorded with what Jaxart had said, that the Dhuvians jealously guarded their scientific weapons from even their allies, the Sarks.

"Besides," Ywain said mockingly, "why should Dhuvian science interest you if you hold the key to the far greater science locked in Rhiannon's tomb?"

"I do hold that key and that secret," Carse told her and his answer took the mockery out of her face.

"What are you going to do with it?" she asked.

"On that," Carse said grimly, "my mind is clear. Whatever power that tomb gives me I'll use against Sark and Caer Dhu— and I hope it's enough to destroy you down to the last stone in your city!"

Ywain nodded. "Well answered. And now—what about me? Will you have me flogged and chained to an oar? Or will you kill me here?"

He shook his head slowly, answering her last question. "I could have let my wolves tear you if I had wished you killed now."

Her teeth showed briefly in what might have been a smile. "Small satisfaction in that. Not like doing it with one's own hands."

"I might have done that too, here in the cabin."

"And you tried, yet did not. Well then—what?"

Carse did not answer. It came to him that, whatever he might do to her, she would still mock him to the very end. There was the steel of pride in this woman.

He had marked her though. The gash on her cheek would heal and fade but never vanish. She would never forget him as long as she lived. He was glad he had marked her.

"No answer?" she mocked. "You're full of indecision for a conqueror."

Carse went around the table to her with a pantherish step. He still did not answer because he did not know. He only knew that he hated her as he had never hated anything in his life before. He bent over her, his face dead white, his hands open and hungry.

She reached up swiftly and found his throat. Her fingers were as strong as steel and the nails bit deep.

He caught her wrists and bent them away, the muscles of his arms standing out like ropes against her strength. She strove against him in silent fury and then suddenly she broke. Her lips parted as she strained for breath, and Carse suddenly set his own lips against them.

There was no love, no tenderness in that kiss. It was a gesture of male contempt, brutal and full of hate. Yet for one strange moment then her sharp teeth had met in his lower lip and his mouth was full of blood and she was laughing.

"You barbarian swine," she whispered. "Now my brand is on you."

He stood looking at her. Then he reached out and caught her by the shoulders and the chair went over with a crash.

"Go ahead," she said. "If it pleases you."

He wanted to break her between his two hands. He wanted . . .

He thrust her from him and went out and he had not passed the door since.

Now he fingered the new scar on his lip and watched her come onto the deck with Boghaz. She stood very straight in her jeweled hauberk but the lines around her mouth were deeper and her eyes, for all their bitter pride, were somber.

He did not go to her. She was left alone with her guard, and Carse could glance at her covertly. It was easy to guess what was in her mind. She was thinking how it felt to stand on the deck of her own ship, a prisoner. She was thinking that the brooding coast ahead was the end of all her voyaging. She was thinking that she was going to die.

The cry came down from the masthead—*"Khondor!"*

Carse saw at first only a great craggy rock that towered high above the surf, a sort of blunt cape between two fiords. Then, from the seemingly barren and uninhabitable place, Sky Folk came flying until the air throbbed with the beating of their wings. Swimmers came also, like a swarm of little comets that left trails of fire in the sea. And from the fiord mouths came longships, smaller than the galley, swift as hornets, with shields along their sides.

The voyage was over. The black galley was escorted with cheers and shouting into Khondor.

Carse understood now what Jaxart had meant. Nature had made a virtually impregnable fortress out of the rock itself, walled in by impassable mountains from land attack, protected by unscalable cliffs from the sea, its only gateway the narrow twisting fiord on the north side. That too was guarded by ballistas which could make the fiord a death trap for any ship that entered it.

The tortuous channel widened at the end into a landlocked harbor that not even the winds could attack. Khond longships, fishing boats and a scattering of foreign craft filled the basin and the black galley glided like a queen among them.

The quays and the dizzy flight of steps that led up to the summit of the rock, connecting on the upper levels with tunneled galleries, were thronged with the people of Khondor and the allied clans that had taken refuge with them. They were a hardy lot with a raffish sturdy look that Carse liked. The cliffs and the mountain peaks flung back their cheering in deafening echoes.

Under cover of the noise Boghaz said urgently to Carse for the hundredth time, "Let me bargain with them for the secret! I can get us each a kingdom—more, if you will!"

And for the hundredth time, Carse answered, "I have not said that I know the secret. If I do it is my own."

Boghaz swore in an ecstasy of frustration and demanded of the gods what he had done to be thus hardly used.

Ywain's eyes turned upon the Earthman once and then away.

Swimmers in their gleaming hundreds, Sky Folk with their proud wings folded—for the first time Carse saw their women, creatures so exquisitely lovely that it hurt to look at them—the tall fair Khonds and the foreign stocks, a kaleidoscope of colors and glinting steel. Mooring lines snaked out, were caught and snubbed around the bollards. The galley came to rest.

Carse led his crew ashore and Ywain walked erect beside him, wearing her shackles as though they were golden ornaments she had chosen to become her.

There was a group standing apart on the quay, waiting. A handful of hard-bitten men who looked as though sea water ran in their veins instead of blood, tough veterans of many battles, some fierce and dark-visaged, some with ruddy laughing faces, one with cheek and sword arm hideously burned and scared.

Among them was a tall Khond with a look of harnessed lightning about him and hair the color of new copper and by his side stood a girl dressed in a blue robe.

Her straight fair hair was bound back by a fillet of plain gold and between her breasts, left bare by the loose outer garment, a single black pearl glowed with lustrous darkness. Her left hand rested on the shoulder of Shallah the Swimmer.

Like all the rest the girl was paying more attention to Ywain than she was to Carse. He realized somewhat bitterly that the whole crowd had gathered less to see the unknown barbarian who had done it all than to see the daughter of Garach of Sark walking in chains.

The red-haired Khond remembered his manners enough to make the sign of peace and say, "I am Rold of Khondor. We, the Sea Kings, make you welcome."

Carse responded but saw that already he was half forgotten in the man's savage pleasure at the plight of his arch-enemy.

They had much to say to each other, Ywain and the Sea Kings.

Carse looked again at the girl. He had heard Jaxart's eager greeting to her and knew now that she was Emer, Rold's sister.

He had never seen anyone like her before. There was a touch of the fey, of the elfin, about her, as though she lived in the human world by courtesy and could leave it any time she chose.

Her eyes were gray and sad, but her mouth was gentle and shaped for laughter. Her body had the same quick grace he had noticed in the Halflings and yet it was a very humanly lovely body.

She had pride, too—pride to match Ywain's own though they were so different. Ywain was all brilliance and fire and passion, a rose with blood-red petals. Carse understood her. He could play her own game and beat her at it.

But he knew that he would never understand Emer. She was part of all the things he had left behind him long ago. She was the lost music and the forgotten dreams, the pity and the tenderness, the whole shadowy world he had glimpsed in childhood but never since.

All at once she looked up and saw him. Her eyes met his—met and held, and would not go away. He saw their expression change. He saw every drop of color drain from her face until it was like a mask of snow. He heard her say,

"Who are you?"

He bent his head. "Lady Emer, I am Carse the barbarian."

He saw how her fingers dug into Shallah's fur and he saw how the Swimmer watched him with her soft hostile gaze. Emer's voice answered, almost below the threshold of hearing.

"You have no name. You are as Shallah said—a stranger."

Something about the way she said the word made it seem full of an eery menace. And it was so uncannily close to the truth.

He sensed suddenly that this girl had the same extra-sensory power as the Halflings, developed in her human brain to even greater strength.

But he forced a laugh. "You must have many strangers in Khondor these days." He glanced at the Swimmer. "Shallah distrusts me, I don't know why. Did she tell you also that I carry a dark shadow with me wherever I go?"

"She did not need to tell me," Emer whispered. "Your face is only a mask and behind it is a darkness and a wish—and they are not of our world."

She came to him with slow steps, as though drawn against her will. He could see the dew of sweat on her forehead and abruptly he began to tremble himself, a shivering deep within him that was not of the flesh.

"I can see . . . I can almost see . . ."

He did not want her to say any more. He did not want to hear it.

"No!" he cried out. "*No!*"

She suddenly fell forward, her body heavy against him. He caught her and eased her down to the gray rock, where she lay in a dead faint.

He knelt helplessly beside her but Shallah said quietly, "I will care for her." He stood up and then Rold and the Sea Kings were around them like a ring of startled eagles.

"The seeing was upon her," Shallah told them.

"But it has never taken her like this before," Rold said worriedly. "What happened? My thought was all on Ywain."

"What happened is between the Lady Emer and the stranger," said Shallah. She picked up the girl in her strong arms and bore her away.

Carse felt that strange inner fear still chilling him. The "seeing" they had called it. Seeing indeed, not of any supernatural kind, but of strong extra-sensory powers that had looked deep into his mind.

In sudden reaction of anger Carse said, "A fine welcome! All of us brushed aside for a look at Ywain and then your sister faints at sight of me!"

"By the gods!" Rold groaned. "Your pardon—we had not meant it so. As for my sister, she is too much with the Halflings and given as they are to dreams of the mind."

He raised his voice, "Ho, there, Ironbeard! Let us redeem our manners!"

The largest of the Sea Kings, a grizzled giant with a laugh like the north wind, came forward and before Carse realized their intention they had tossed him onto their shoulders and marched with him up the quay where everyone could see him.

"Hark, you!" Rold bellowed. "*Hark!*"

The crowd quieted at his voice.

"Here is Carse, the barbarian. He took the galley—he captured Ywain—he slew the Serpent! How do you greet him?"

Their greeting nearly brought down the cliffs. The two big men bore Carse up the steps and would not put him down. The people of Khondor streamed after them, accepting the men of his crew as their brothers. Carse caught a glimpse of Boghaz, his face one vast porcine smile, holding a giggling girl in each arm.

Ywain walked alone in the center of a guard of the Sea Kings. The scarred man watched her with a brooding madness in his unwinking eyes.

Rold and Ironbeard dumped Carse to his feet at the summit, panting.

"You're a heavyweight, my friend," gasped Rold, grinning. "Now—does our penance satisfy you?"

Carse swore, feeling shamefaced. Then he stared in wonder at the city of Khondor.

A monolithic city, hewn in the rock itself. The crest had been split, apparently by diastrophic convulsions in the remoter ages of Mars. All along the inner cliffs of the split were doorways and the openings of galleries, a perfect honeycomb of dwellings and giddy flights of steps.

Those who had been too old or disabled to climb the long way down to the harbor cheered them now from the galleries or from the narrow streets and squares.

The sea wind blew keen and cold at this height, so that there was always a throb and a wail in the streets of Khondor, mingling with the booming voices of the waves below. From the upper crags there was a coming and going of the Sky Folk, who seemed to like the high places as though the streets cramped them. Their fledglings tossed on the wind, swooping and tumbling in their private games, with bursts of elfin laughter.

Landward, Carse looked down upon green fields and pasture land, locked tight in the arms of the mountains. It seemed as though this place could withstand a siege forever.

They went along the rocky ways with the people of Khondor pouring after them, filling the eyrie-city with shouts and laughter. There was a large square, with two squat strong porticoes facing each other across it. One had carven pillars before it, dedicated to the God of Waters and the God of the Four Winds. Before the other a golden banner whipped, broidered with the eagle of Khondor.

At the threshold of the palace Ironbeard clapped the Earthman on the shoulder, a staggering buffet.

"There'll be heavy talk along with the feasting of the Council tonight. But we have plenty of time to get decently drunk before that. How say you?"

And Carse said, "Lead on!"

CHAPTER ELEVEN

Dread Accusation

THAT NIGHT TORCHES lighted the banquet hall with a smoky glare. Fires burned on round hearths between the pillars, which were hung with shields and the ensigns of many ships. The whole vast room was hollowed out of the living rock with galleries that gave upon the sea.

Long tables were set out. Servants ran among them with flagons of wine and smoking joints fresh from the fires. Carse had nobly followed the lead of Ironbeard all afternoon and to his somewhat unsteady sight it seemed that all of Khondor was feasting there to the wild music of harps and the singing of the skalds.

He sat with the Sea Kings and the leaders of the Swimmers and the Sky Folk on the raised dais at the north end of the hall. Ywain was there also. They had made her stand and she had remained motionless for hours, giving no sign of weakness, her head still high. Carse admired her. He liked it in her that she was still the proud Ywain.

Around the curving wall had been set the figureheads of ships taken in war so that Carse felt surrounded by shadowy looming monsters that quivered on the brink of life, with the torchlight picking glints from a jeweled eye or a gilded talon, momentarily lighting a carven face half ripped away by a ram.

Emer was nowhere in the hall.

Carse's head rang with the wine and the talking and there was a mounting of excitement in him. He fondled the hilt of the sword of Rhiannon where it lay between his knees. Presently, presently, it would be time.

Rold set his drinking horn down with a bang.

"Now," he said, "let's get to business." He was a trifle thick-tongued, as they all were, but fully in command of himself. "And the business, my lords? Why, a very pleasant one." He laughed. "One we've thought on for a long time, all of us—the death of Ywain of Sark!"

Carse stiffened. He had been expecting that. "Wait! She's my captive."

They all cheered him at that and drank his health again, all except Thorn of Tarak, the man with the useless arm and the twisted cheek, who had sat silent all evening, drinking steadily but not getting drunk.

"Of course," said Rold. "Therefore the choice is yours." He turned to look at Ywain with pleasant speculation. "How shall she die?"

"Die?" Carse got to his feet. "What is this talk of Ywain dying?"

They stared at him rather stupidly, too astonished for the moment to believe that they had heard him right. Ywain smiled grimly.

"But why else did you bring her here?" demanded Ironbeard. "The sword is too clean a death or you would have slain her on the galley. Surely you gave her to us for our vengeance?"

"I have not given her to anyone!" Carse shouted. "I say she is mine and I say she is not to be killed!"

There was a stunned pause. Ywain's eyes met the Earthman's, bright with mockery. Then Thorn of Tarak said one word, "*Why?*"

He was looking straight at Carse now with his dark mad eyes and the Earthman found his question hard to answer.

"Because her life is worth too much, as a hostage. Are you babes, that you can't see that? Why, you could buy the release of every Khond slave—perhaps even bring Sark to terms!"

Thorn laughed. It was not pleasant laughter.

The leader of the Swimmers said, "My people would not have it so."

"Nor mine," said the winged man.

"Nor mine!" Rold was on his feet now, flushed with anger. "You're an outlander, Carse. Perhaps you don't understand how things are with us!"

"No," said Thorn of Tarak softly. "Give her back. She, that learned kindness at Garach's knee, and drank wisdom from the teachers of Caer Dhu. Set her free again to mark others with her blessing as she marked me when she burned my longship." His eyes burned into the Earthman. "Let her live—because the barbarian loves her."

Carse stared at him. He knew vaguely that the Sea Kings tensed forward, watching him—the nine chiefs of war with the eyes of tigers, their hands already on their sword hilts. He knew that Ywain's lips curved as though at some private jest. And he burst out laughing.

He roared with it. "Look you!" he cried, and turned his back so that they might see the scars of the lash. "Is that a love note Ywain has written on my hide? And if it were—it was no song of passion the Dhuvian was singing me when I slew him!"

He swung round again, hot with wine, flushed with the power he knew he had over them.

"Let any man of you say that again and I'll take the head from his shoulders. Look at you. Great nidderlings, quarreling over a wench's life! Why don't you gather, all of you, and make an assault of Sark!"

There was a great clatter and scraping of feet as they rose, howling at him in their rage at his impudence, bearded chins thrust forward, knotty fists hammering on the board.

"What do you take yourself for, you pup of the sandhills?" Rold shouted. "Have you never heard of the Dhuvians and their weapons, who are Sark's allies? How many Khonds do you think have died these long years past, trying to face those weapons?"

"But suppose," asked Carse, "you had weapons of your own?"

Something in his voice penetrated even to Rold, who scowled at him.

"If you have a meaning, speak it plainly!"

"Sark could not stand against you," Carse said, "if you had the weapons of Rhiannon."

Ironbeard snorted. "Oh, aye, the Cursed One! Find his Tomb and the powers in it and we'll follow you to Sark, fast enough."

"Then you have pledged yourselves," Carse said and held the sword aloft. "Look there! Look well—does any man among you know enough to recognize this blade?"

Thorn of Tarak reached out his one good hand and drew the sword closer that he might study it. Then his hand began to tremble. He looked up at the others and said in a strange awed voice, "It is the sword of Rhiannon."

A harsh sibilance of indrawn breath and then Carse spoke.

"There is my proof. I hold the secret of the Tomb."

Silence. Then a guttural sound from Ironbeard and after that, mounting, wild excitement that burst and spread like flame.

"He knows the secret! By the gods he *knows!*"

"Would you face the Dhuvian weapons if you had the greater powers of Rhiannon?" Carse asked.

There was a such a crazy clamor of excitement that it took moments for Rold's voice to be heard. The tall Khond's face was half doubtful.

"Could we use Rhiannon's weapons of power if we had them? We can't even understand the Dhuvian weapons you captured in the galley."

"Give me time to study and test them and I'll solve the way of using Rhiannon's instruments of power," Carse replied confidently.

He was sure that he could. It would take time but he was sure that his own knowledge of science was sufficient to decipher the operation of at least some of those weapons of an alien science.

He swung the great sword high, glittering in the red light of the torches, and his voice rang out, "And if I arm you thus will you make good your word? Will you follow me to Sark?"

All doubts were swept away by the challenge, by the heaven-sent opportunity to strike at last at Sark on at least even terms.

The answer of the Sea Kings roared out. "We'll follow!"

It was then that Carse saw Emer. She had come onto the dais by some inner passage, standing now between two brooding giant figureheads crusted with the memory of the sea, and her eyes were fixed on Carse, wide and full of horror.

Something about her compelled them, even in that moment, to turn and stare. She stepped out into the open space above in the table. She wore only a loose white robe and her hair was unbound. It was as though she had just risen from sleep and was walking still in the midst of a dream.

But it was an evil dream. The weight of it crushed her, so that her steps were slow and her breathing labored and even these fighting men felt the touch of it on their own hearts.

Emer spoke and her words were very clear and measured.

"I saw this before when the stranger first came before me, but my strength failed me and I could not speak. Now I shall tell you. You must destroy this man. He is danger, he is darkness, he is death for us all!"

Ywain stiffened, her eyes narrowing. Carse felt her glance on him, intense with interest. But his attention was all on Emer. As on the quay he was filled with a strange terror that had nothing to do with ordinary fear, an unexplainable dread of this girl's strong extra-sensory powers.

Rold broke in and Carse got a grip on himself. Fool, he thought, to be upset by woman's talk, woman's imaginings . . .

"—the secret of the Tomb!" Rold was saying. "Did you not hear? He can give us the power of Rhiannon!"

"Aye," said Emer somberly. "I heard and I believe. He knows well the hidden place of the Tomb and he knows the weapons that are there."

She moved closer, looking up at Carse where he stood in the torchlight, the sword in his hands. She spoke now directly to him.

"Why should you not know, who have brooded there so long in the darkness? Why should you not know, who made those powers of evil with your own hands?"

Was it the heat and the wine that made the rock walls reel and put the cold sickness in his belly? He tried to speak and only a hoarse sound came, without words. Emer's voice went on, relentless, terrible.

"*Why should you not know—you who are the Cursed One, Rhiannon!*"

The rock walls gave back the word like a whispered curse, until the hall was filled with the ghostly name *Rhiannon!* It seemed to Carse that the very shields rang with it and the banners trembled. And still the girl stood unmoving, challenging him to speak, and his tongue was dead and dry in his mouth.

They stared at him, all of them—Ywain and the Sea Kings and the feasters silent amid the spilled wine and the forgotten banquet.

It was as though he were Lucifer fallen, crowned with all the wickedness of the world.

Then Ywain laughed, a sound with an odd note of triumph in it. "So that is why! I see it now—why you called upon the Cursed One in the cabin there, when you stood against the power of Caer Dhu that no man can resist, and slew S'San."

Her voice rang out mockingly. "Hail, Lord Rhiannon!"

That broke the spell. Carse said, "You lying vixen. You salve your pride with that. No mere man could down Ywain of Sark but a god—that's different."

He shouted at them all. "Are you fools or children that you listen to such madness? You, there, Jaxart—you toiled beside me at the oar. Does a god bleed under the lash like a common slave?"

Jaxart said slowly, "That first night in the galley I heard you cry Rhiannon's name."

Carse swore. He rounded on the Sea Kings. "You're warriors, not serving maids. Use your wits. Has my body mouldered in a tomb for ages? Am I a dead thing walking?"

Out of the tail of his eyes he saw Boghaz moving toward the dais and here and there the drunken devils of the galley's crew were rising also, loosening their swords, to rally to him.

Rold put his hands on Emer's shoulders and said sternly, "What say you to this, my sister?"

"I have not spoken of the body," Emer answered, "only of the mind. The mind of the mighty Cursed One could live on and on.

It did live and now it has somehow entered into this barbarian, dwelling there as a snail lies curled within its shell."

She turned again to Carse. "In yourself you are alien and strange and for that alone I would fear because I do not understand. But for that alone I would not wish you dead. But I say that Rhiannon watches through your eyes and speaks with your tongue, that in your hands are his sword and scepter. And therefore I ask your death."

Carse said harshly, "Will you listen to this crazy child?"

But he saw the deep doubt in their faces. The superstitious fools! There was real danger here.

Carse looked at his gathering men, figuring his chances of fighting clear if he had to. He mentally cursed the yellow-haired witch who had spoken this incredible, impossible madness.

Madness, yes. And yet the quivering fear in his own heart had crystallized into a single stabbing shaft.

"If I were possessed," he snarled, "would I not be the first to know?"

"Would I not?" echoed the question in Carse's brain. And memories came rushing back—the nightmare darkness of the Tomb, where he had seemed to feel an eager alien presence, and the dreams and the half-remembered knowledge that was not his own.

It was not true. It could not be true. He would not let it be true.

Boghaz came up onto the dais. He gave Carse one queer shrewd glance but when he spoke to the Sea Kings his manner was smoothly diplomatic.

"No doubt the Lady Emer has wisdom far beyond mine and I mean her no disrespect. However, the barbarian is my friend and I speak from my own knowledge. He is what he says, no more and no less."

The men of the galleys crew growled a warning assent to that.

Boghaz continued. "Consider, my lords. Would Rhiannon slay a Dhuvian and make war on the Sarks? Would he offer victory to Khondor?"

"No!" said Ironbeard. "By the gods, he wouldn't. He was all for the Serpent's spawn."

Emer spoke, demanding their attention. "My lords, have I ever lied or advised you wrongly?"

They shook their heads and Rold said. "No. But your word is not enough in this."

"Very well, forget my word. There is a way to prove whether or not he is Rhiannon. Let him pass the testing before the Wise Ones."

Rold pulled at his beard, scowling. Then he nodded. "Wisely said," he agreed, and the others joined in.

Rold turned to Carse. "You will submit?"

"No," Carse answered furiously. "I will not. To the devil with all such superstitious flummery! If my offer of the Tomb isn't enough to convince you of where I stand—why, you can do without it and without me."

Rold's face hardened. "No harm will come to you. If you're not Rhiannon you have nothing to fear. Again will you submit?"

"*No!*"

He began to stride back along the table toward his men, who were already bunched together like wolves snarling for a fight. But Thorn of Tarak caught his ankle as he passed and brought him down and the men of Khondor swarmed over the galley's crew, disarming them before blood was shed.

Carse struggled like a wildcat among the Sea Kings, in a brief passion of fury that lasted until Ironbeard struck him regretfully on the head with a brass-bound drinking horn.

CHAPTER TWELVE

The Cursed One

THE DARKNESS LIFTED slowly. Carse was conscious first of sounds—the suck and sigh of water close at hand, the muffled roaring of surf beyond a wall of rock. Otherwise it was still and heavy.

Light came next, a suffused soft glow. When he opened his eyes he saw high above him a rift of stars and below that was arching rock, crusted with crystalline deposits that gave back a gentle gleaming.

He was in a sea cave, a grotto floored with a pool of milky flame. As his sight cleared he saw that there was a ledge on the opposite side of the pool, with steps leading down from above. The Sea Kings stood there with shackled Ywain and Boghaz and the chief men of the Swimmers and the Sky Folk. All watched him and none spoke.

Carse found that he was bound upright to a thin spire of rock, quite alone.

Emer stood before him, waist deep in the pool. The black pearl gleamed between her breasts, and the bright water ran like a spilling of diamonds from her hair. In her hands she held a great rough jewel, dull gray in color and cloudy as though it slept.

When she saw that his eyes were open she said clearly, "Come, oh my masters! It is time."

A regretful sigh murmured through the grotto. The surface of the pool was disturbed with a trembling of phosphorescence and the waters parted smoothly as three shapes swam slowly to Emer's side. They were the heads of three Swimmers, white with age.

Their eyes were the most awful things that Carse had ever seen. For they were young with an alien sort of youth that was not of the body and in them was a wisdom and a strength that frightened him.

He strained against his bonds, still half dazed from Ironbeard's blow, and he heard above him a rustling as of great birds roused from slumber.

Looking up he saw on the shadowy ledges three brooding figures, the old, old eagles of the Sky Folk with tired wings, and in their faces too was the light of wisdom divorced from flesh.

He found his tongue, then. He raged and struggled to be free and his voice had a hollow empty sound in the quiet vault and they did not answer and his bonds were tight.

He realized at last that it was no use. He leaned breathless and shaken, against the spire of rock.

A harsh cracked whisper came then from the ledge above. "Little sister—lift up the stone of thought."

Emer raised the cloudy jewel in her hands.

It was an eery thing to watch. Carse did not understand at first. Then he saw that as the eyes of Emer and the Wise Ones grew dim and veiled the cloudy gray of the jewel cleared and brightened.

It seemed that all the power of their minds was pouring into the focal point of the crystal, blending through it into one strong beam. And he felt the pressure of those gathered minds upon his own mind!

Carse sensed dimly what they were doing. The thoughts of the conscious mind were a tiny electric pulsation through the neurons. That electric pulse could be dampened, neutralized, by a stronger counter-impulse such as they were focusing on him through that electro-sensitive crystal.

They themselves could not know the basic science behind their attack upon his mind! These Halflings, strong in extra-sensory powers, had perhaps long ago discovered that the crystal could focus their minds together and had used the discovery without ever knowing its scientific basis.

"But I can hold them off," Carse whispered thickly to himself. "I can hold them all off!"

It enraged him, that calm impersonal beating down of his mind. He fought it with all the force within him but it was not enough.

And then, as before when he had faced the singing stars of the Dhuvian, some force in him that did not seem his own came to aid him.

It built a barrier against the Wise Ones and held it, held it until Carse moaned in agony. Sweat ran down his face and his body writhed and he knew dimly that he was going to die, that he couldn't stand any more.

His mind was like a closed room that is suddenly burst open by contending winds that turn over the piled-up memories and shake the dusty dreams and reveal everything, even in the darkest corners.

All except one. One place where the shadow was solid and impenetrable, and would not be dispersed.

The jewel blazed between Emer's hands. And there was a stillness like the silence in the spaces between the stars.

Emer's voice rang clear across it.

"Rhiannon, *speak!*"

The dark shadow that Carse felt laired in his mind quivered, stirred but gave no other sign. He felt that it waited and watched.

The silence pulsed. Across the pool, the watchers on the ledge moved uneasily.

Boghaz' voice came querulously. "It is madness! How can this barbarian be the Cursed One of long ago?"

But Emer paid no heed and the jewel in her hand blazed higher and higher.

"The Wise Ones have strength, Rhiannon! They can break this man's mind. They *will* break it unless you speak!"

And savagely triumphant now, "What will you do then? Creep into another man's brain and body? You cannot, Rhiannon! For you would have done so ere now if you could!"

Across the pool Ironbeard said hoarsely, "I do not like this!"

But Emer went mercilessly on and now her voice seemed the only thing in Carse's universe—relentless, terrible.

"The man's mind is cracking, Rhiannon. A minute more—a minute more and your only instrument becomes a helpless idiot. Speak now, if you would save him!"

Her voice rang and echoed from the vaulting rock of the cavern and the jewel in her hands was a living flame of force.

Carse felt the agony that convulsed that crouching shadow in his mind—agony of doubt, of fear—

And then suddenly that dark shadow seemed to explode through all Carse's brain and body, to possess him utterly in every atom. And he heard his own voice, alien in tone and timbre, shouting, *"Let the man's mind live! I will speak!"*

The thunderous echoes of that terrible cry died slowly and in the pregnant hush that followed Emer gave back one step and then another, as though her very flesh recoiled.

The jewel in her hands dimmed suddenly. Fiery ripples broke and fled as the Swimmers shrank away and the wings of the Sky Folk clashed against the rock. In the eyes of all of them was the light of realization and of fear.

From the rigid figures that watched across the water, from Rold and the Sea Kings, came a shivering sigh that was a name.

"Rhiannon! The Cursed One!"

It came to Carse that even Emer, who had dared to force into the open the hidden thing she had sensed in his mind, was afraid of the thing now that she had evoked it.

And he, Matthew Carse, was afraid. He had known fear before. But even the terror he had felt when he faced the Dhuvian was nothing to this blind shuddering agony.

Dreams, illusions, the figments of an obsessed mind—he had tried to believe that that was what these hints of strangeness were. But not now. Not now! He knew the truth and it was a terrible thing to know.

"It proves nothing!" Boghaz was wailing insistently. "You have hypnotized him, made him admit the impossible."

"It is Rhiannon," whispered one of the Swimmers. She raised her white-furred shoulders from the water, her ancient hands lifted. "It is Rhiannon in the stranger's body."

And then, in a chilling cry, "Kill the man before the Cursed One uses him to destroy us all!"

A hellish clamor broke instantly from the echoing walls as an ancient dread screamed from human and Halfling throats.

"Kill him! Kill!"

Carse, helpless himself but one in feeling with the dark thing within him, felt that dark one's wild anxiety. He heard the ringing voice that was not his own shouting out above the clamor.

"Wait! You are afraid because I am Rhiannon! But I have not come back to harm you!"

"Why have you come back then?" whispered Emer.

She was looking into Carse's face. And by her dilated eyes Carse knew that his face must be strange and awful to look upon.

Through Carse's lips, Rhiannon answered, "I have come to redeem my sin—I swear it!"

Emer's white, shaken face flashed burning hate. "Oh, father of lies! Rhiannon, who brought evil on our world by giving the Serpent power, who was condemned and punished for his crime—Rhiannon, the Cursed One, turned saint!"

She laughed, a bitter laughter born of hate and fear, that was picked up by the Swimmers and the Sky Folk.

"For your own sake you must believe me!" raged the voice of Rhiannon. "Will you not even listen?"

Carse felt the passion of the dark being who had used him in this unholy fashion. He was one with that alien heart that was violent and bitter and yet lonely—lonely as no other could understand the word.

"Listen to Rhiannon?" cried Emer. "Did the Quiru listen long ago? They judged you for your sin!"

"Will you deny me the chance to redeem myself?" The Cursed One's tone was almost pleading. "Can you not understand that this man Carse is my only chance to undo what I did?"

His voice rushed on, urgent, eager. "For an age, I lay fixed and frozen in an imprisonment that not even the pride of Rhiannon could withstand. I realized my sin. I wished to undo it but could not.

"Then into my tomb and prison from outside came this man Carse. I fitted the immaterial electric web of my mind into his brain. I could not dominate him, for his brain was alien and different. But I could influence him a little and I thought that I could act through him.

"For his body was not bound in that place. In him my mind at least could leave it. And in him I left it, not daring to let even him know that I was within his brain.

"I thought that through him I might find a way to crush the Serpent whom I raised from the dust to my sorrow long ago."

Rold's shaking voice cut across the passionate pleading that came from Carse's lips. There was a wild look on the Khond's face. "Emer, let the Cursed One speak no longer! Lift the spell of your minds from the man!"

"Lift the spell!" echoed Ironbeard hoarsely.

"Yes," whispered Emer. "Yes."

Once again the jewel was raised and now the Wise Ones gathered all their strength, spurred by the terror that was on them. The electro-sensitive crystal blazed and it seemed to Carse like bale-fire searing his mind. For Rhiannon fought against it, fought with the desperation of madness.

"You must listen! You must believe!"

"No!" said Emer. "Be silent! Release the man or he will die!"

One last wild protest, broken short by the iron purpose of the Wise Ones. A moment of hesitation—a stab of pain too deep for human understanding—and then the barrier was gone.

The alien presence, the unholy sharing of the flesh, were gone and the mind of Matthew Carse closed over the shadow and hid it. The voice of Rhiannon was stilled.

Like a dead man Carse sagged against his bonds. The light went out of the crystal. Emer let her hands fall. Her head bent forward so that her bright hair veiled her face and the Wise

Ones covered their faces also and remained motionless. The Sea Kings, Ywain, even Boghaz, were held speechless, like men who have narrowly escaped destruction and only realized later how close death has come.

Carse moaned once. For a long time that and his harsh gasping breath were the only sounds.

Then Emer said, "The man must die."

There was nothing in her now but weariness and a grim truth. Carse heard dimly Rold's heavy answer.

"Aye. There is no other way."

Boghaz would have spoken but they silenced him.

Carse said thickly, "It isn't true. Such things can't be."

Emer raised her head and looked at him. Her attitude had changed. She seemed to have no fear of Carse himself, only pity for him.

"Yet you know that it is true."

Carse was silent. He knew.

"You have done no wrong, stranger," she said. "In your mind I saw many things that are strange to me, much that I cannot understand, but there was no evil there. Yet Rhiannon lives in you and we dare not let him live."

"But he can't control me!" Carse made an effort to stand, lifting his head so that he should be heard, for his voice was drained of strength like his body.

"You heard him admit that himself. He cannot dominate me. My will is my own."

Ywain said slowly, "What of S'San, and the sword? It was not the mind of Carse the barbarian that controlled you then."

"He cannot master you," said Emer, "except when the barriers of your own mind weaken under stress. Great fear or pain or weariness—perhaps even the unconsciousness of sleep or wine—might give the Cursed One his chance and then it would be too late."

Rold said, "We dare not take the risk."

"But I can give the secret of Rhiannon's Tomb!" cried Carse.

He saw that thought begin to work in their minds and he went on, the ghastly unfairness of the whole thing acting as a spur.

"Do you call this justice, you men of Khondor who cry out against the Sarks? Will you condemn me when you know I'm innocent? Are you such cowards that you'll doom your people to live forever under the dragon's claws because of a shadow out of the past?

"Let me lead you to the Tomb. Let me give you victory. That will prove I have no part with Rhiannon!"

Boghaz' mouth fell open in horror. "No, Carse, no! Don't *give* it to them!"

Rold shouted, "Silence!"

Ironbeard laughed grimly. "Let the Cursed One lay his hands upon his weapons? That would be madness indeed!"

"Very well," said Carse. "Let Rold go. I'll map the way for him. Keep me here. Guard me. That should be safe enough. You can kill me swiftly if Rhiannon takes control of me."

He caught them with that. The only thing greater than their hate and dread of the Cursed One was their burning desire for the legendary weapons of power that might in time mean victory and freedom for Khondor.

They pondered, doubtful, hesitating. But he knew their decision even before Rold turned and said, "We accept, Carse. It would be safer to slay you out of hand but—we need those weapons."

Carse felt the cold presence of imminent death withdraw a little. He warned, "It won't be easy. The tomb is near Jekkara."

Ironbeard asked, "What of Ywain?"

"Death and at once!" said Thorn of Tarak harshly.

Ywain stood silent, looking at them all with cool, careless unconcern.

But Emer interposed. "Rold goes into danger. Until he returns safely let Ywain be kept in case we need a hostage for him."

It was only now that Carse saw Boghaz in the shadows, shaking his head in misery, tears running down his fat cheeks.

"He *gives* them a secret worth a kingdom!" wailed Boghaz. "I have been robbed!"

CHAPTER THIRTEEN
Catastrophe

THE DAYS THAT followed after that were long strange days for Matthew Carse. He drew a map from memory of the hills above Jekkara and the place of the tomb, and Rold studied it until he knew it as he knew his own courtyard. Then the parchment was burned.

Rold took one longship and a picked crew, and left Khondor by night. Jaxart went with him. Everyone knew the dangers of that voyage. But one swift ship, with Swimmers to scout the way, might elude the Sark patrols. They would beach in a hidden cove Jaxart knew of, west of Jekkara, and go the rest of the way overland.

"If aught goes wrong on the return," Rold said grimly, "we'll sink our ship at once."

After the longship sailed there was nothing to do but wait.

Carse was never alone. He was given three small rooms in a disused part of the palace and guards were with him always.

A corroding fear crept in his mind, no matter how he fought it down. He caught himself listening for an inner voice to speak, watching for some small sign or gesture that was not his own. The horror of the ordeal in the place of the Wise Ones had left its mark. He knew now. And, knowing, he could never for one moment forget.

It was not fear of death that oppressed him, though he was human and did not want to die. It was dread of living again through that moment when he had ceased to be himself, when his mind and body were possessed in every cell by the invader. Worse than the dread of madness was the uncanny fear of Rhiannon's domination.

Emer came again and again to talk with him and study him. He knew she was watching him for signs of Rhiannon's resurgence. But as long as she smiled he knew that he was safe.

She would not look into his mind again. But she referred once to what she had seen there.

"You come from another world," she said with quiet sureness. "I think I knew that when first I saw you. The memories of it were in your mind—a desolate, desert place, very strange and sad."

They were on his tiny balcony, high under the crest of the rock, and the wind blew clean and strong down from the green forests.

Carse nodded. "A bitter world. But it had its own beauty."

"There is beauty even in death," said Emer, "but I am glad to be alive."

"Let's forget that other place, then. Tell me of this one that lives so strongly. Rold said you were much with the Halflings."

She laughed. "He chides me sometimes, saying that I am a changeling and not human at all."

"You don't look human now," Carse told her, "with the moonlight on your face and your hair all tangled with it."

"Sometimes I wish it were true. You have never been to the Isles of the Sky Folk?"

"No."

"They're like castles rising from the sea, almost as tall as Khondor. When the Sky Folk take me there I feel the lack of wings, for I must be carried or remain on the ground while they soar and swoop around me. It seems to me then that flying is the most beautiful thing in the world and I weep because I can never know it.

"But when I go with the Swimmers I am happier. My body is much like theirs, though never quite so fleet. And it is wonderful—oh, wonderful—to plunge down into the glowing waters and see the gardens that they keep, with the strange sea-flowers bowing to the tide and the little bright fish darting like birds among them.

"And their cities, silver bubbles in the shallow ocean. The heavens there are all glowing fire, bright gold when the sun shines, silver at night. It is always warm and the air is still and there are little ponds where the babies play, learning to be strong for the open sea.

"I have learned much from the Halflings," she finished.

"But the Dhuvians are Halflings too?" Carse said.

Emer shivered. "The Dhuvians are the oldest of the Halfling races. There are but few of them now and those all dwell at Caer Dhu."

Carse asked suddenly, "You have Halfling wisdom—is there no way to be rid of the monstrous thing within me?"

She answered somberly, "Not even the Wise Ones have learned that much."

The Earthman's fists closed savagely on the rock of the gallery.

"It would have been better if you'd killed me there in the cave!"

Emer put her gentle hand on his and said, "There is always time for death."

After she left him Carse paced the floor for hours, wanting the release of wine and not daring to take it, afraid to sleep. When exhaustion took him at last, his guards strapped him to his bed and one stood by with a drawn sword and watched, ready to wake him instantly if he should seem to dream.

And he did dream. Sometimes they were nothing more than nightmares born of his own anguish, and sometimes the dark whisper of an alien voice came gliding into his mind, saying *"Do not be afraid. Let me speak, for I must tell you."*

Many times Carse awoke with the echo of his screaming in his ears, and the sword's point at his throat.

"I mean no harm or evil. I can stop your fears if you will only listen!"

Carse wondered which he would do first—go mad or fling himself from the balcony into the sea.

Boghaz clung closer to him than ever. He seemed fascinated by the thing that lurked in Carse. He was awed too but not too much awed to be furious over the disposal of the Tomb.

"I told you to let me bargain for it!" he would say. "The greatest source of power on Mars and you give it away! Give it without even exacting a promise that they won't kill you when they get it."

His fat hands made a gesture of finality. "I repeat, you have robbed me, Carse. Robbed me of my kingdom."

And Carse, for once, was glad of the Valkisian's effrontery because it kept him from being alone. Boghaz would sit, drinking enormous quantities of wine, and every so often he would look at Carse and chuckle.

"People always said that I had a devil in me. But you, Carse— you have *the* devil in you!"

"Let me speak, Carse, and I will make you understand!"

Carse grew gaunt and hollow-eyed. His face twitched and his hands were unsteady.

Then the news came, brought by a winged man who flew exhausted into Khondor.

It was Emer who told Carse what had happened. She did not really need to. The moment he saw her face, white as death, he knew.

"Rold never reached the Tomb," she said. "A Sark patrol caught him on the outward voyage. They say Rold tried to slay himself to keep the secret safe but he was prevented. They have taken him to Sark."

"But the Sarks don't even know that he has the secret," Carse protested, clutching at that straw, and Emer shook her head.

"They're not fools. They'll want to know the plans of Khondor and why he was bound toward Jekkara with a single ship. They'll have the Dhuvians question him."

Carse realized sickly what that mean. The Dhuvians' hypnotic science had almost conquered his own stubbornly alien brain. It would soon suck all Rold's secrets out of him.

"Then there is no hope?"

"No hope," said Emer. "Not now nor ever again."

They were silent for a while. The wind moaned in the gallery, and the waves rolled in solemn thunder against the cliffs below.

Carse said, "What will be done now?"

"The Sea Kings have sent word through all the free coasts and isles. Every ship and every man is gathering here now and Ironbeard will lead them on to Sark.

"There is little time. Even when the Dhuvians have the secret it will take them time to go to the Tomb and bring the weapons back and learn their use. If we can crush Sark before then . . .

"*Can* you crush Sark?" asked Carse.

She answered honestly. "No. The Dhuvians will intervene and even the weapons they already have will turn the scale against us.

"But we must try and die trying, for it will be a better death than the one that will come after when Sark and the Serpent level Khondor into the sea."

He stood looking down at her and it seemed to him that no moment of his life had been more bitter than this.

"Will the Sea Kings take me with them?"

Stupid question. He knew the answer before she gave it to him.

"They are saying now that this was all a trick of Rhiannon's, misleading Rold to get the secret into Caer Dhu. I have told them it was not so but—"

She made a small tired gesture and turned her head away. "Ironbeard, I think, believes me. He will see that your death is swift and clean."

After a while Carse said, "And Ywain?"

"Thorn of Tarak has arranged that. Her they will take with them to Sark, lashed to the bow of the leader's ship."

There was another silence. It seemed to Carse that the very air was heavy, so that it weighed upon his heart.

He found that Emer had left silently. He turned and went out onto the little gallery, where he stood staring down at the sea.

"Rhiannon," he whispered, "I curse you. I curse the night I saw your sword and I curse the day I came to Khondor with the promise of your tomb."

The light was fading. The sea was like a bath of blood in the sunset. The wind brought him broken shouts and cries from the city and far below longships raced into the fiord.

Carse laughed mirthlessly. "You've got what you wanted," he told the Presence within him, "but you won't enjoy it long!"

Small triumph.

The strain of the past few days and this final shock were too much for any man to take. Carse sat down on the carven bench and put his head between his hands and stayed that way, too weary even for emotion.

The voice of the dark invader whispered in his brain and for the first time Carse was too numb to fight it down.

"I might have saved you this if you had listened. Fools and children, all of you, that you would not listen!"

"Very well then—speak," Carse muttered heavily. "The evil is done now and Ironbeard will be here soon. I give you leave, Rhiannon. Speak."

And he did, flooding Carse's mind with the voice of thought, raging like a storm wind trapped in a narrow vault, desperate, pleading.

"If you'll trust me, Carse, I could still save Khondor. Lend me your body, let me use it—"

"I'm not far gone enough for that, even now."

"Gods above!" Rhiannon's thought raged. *"And there's so little time—"*

Carse could sense how he fought to master his fury and when the thought-voice came again it was controlled and quiet with a terrible sincerity.

"I told you the truth in the grotto. You were in my Tomb, Carse. How long do you think I could lie there alone in the dreadful darkness outside space and time and not be changed? I'm no god! Whatever you may call us now we Quiru were never gods—only a race of men who came before the other men.

"They call me evil, the Cursed One—but I was not! Vain and proud, yes, and a fool, but not wicked in intent. I taught the Serpent Folk because they were clever and flattered me—and when they used my

teaching to work evil I tried to stop them and failed because they had learned defenses from me and even my power could not reach them in Caer Dhu.

"Therefore my brother Quiru judged me. They condemned me to remain imprisoned beyond space and time, in the place which they prepared, as long as the fruits of my sin endured on this world. Then they left me.

"We were the last of our race. There was nothing to hold them here, nothing they could do. They wanted only peace and learning. So they went along the path they had chosen. And I waited. Can you think what that waiting must have been?"

"I think you deserved it," Carse said thickly. He was suddenly tense. The shadow, the beginning of a hope . . .

Rhiannon went on. *"I did. But you gave me the chance to undo my sin, to be free to follow my brothers."*

The thought-voice rose with a passion that was strong, dangerously strong.

"Lend me your body, Carse! Lend me your body, that I may do it!"

"No!" cried Carse. *"No!"*

He sprang up, conscious now of his peril, fighting with all his strength against that wild demanding force. He thrust it back, closing his mind against it.

"You cannot master me," he whispered. "You cannot!"

"No," sighed Rhiannon bitterly, *"I cannot."*

And the inner voice was gone.

Carse leaned against the rock, sweating and shaken but fired by a last, desperate hope. No more than an idea, really, but enough to spur him on. Better anything than this waiting for death like a mouse in a trap.

If the gods of chance would only give him a little time . . .

From inside he heard the opening of the door and the challenge of the guards, and his heart sank. He stood breathless, listening for the voice of Ironbeard.

CHAPTER FOURTEEN
Daring Deception

BUT IT WAS not Ironbeard who spoke. It was Boghaz, it was Boghaz alone who came out onto the balcony, very downcast and sad.

"Emer sent me," he said. "She told me the tragic news and I had to come to say good-by."

He took Carse's hand. "The Sea Kings are holding their last council of war before starting for Sark but it will not be long. Old friend, we have been through much together. You have grown to be like my own brother and this parting wrings my heart."

The fat Valkisian seemed genuinely affected. There were tears in his eyes as he looked at Carse.

"Yes, like my own brother, " he repeated unsteadily. "Like brothers, we have quarreled but we have shed blood together too. A man does not forget."

He drew a long sigh. "I should like to have something of yours to keep by me, friend. Some small trinket for memory's sake. Your jeweled collar, perhaps—your belt—you will not miss them now and I should cherish them all the days of my life."

He wiped a tear away and Carse took him not too gently by the throat.

"You hypocritical scoundrel!" he snarled into the Valkisian's startled ear. "A small trinket, eh? By the gods, for a moment you had me fooled!"

"But, my friend—" squeaked Boghaz.

Carse shook him once and let him go. In a rapid undertone he said, "I'm not going to break your heart yet if I can help it. Listen, Boghaz. How would you like to gain back the power of the Tomb?"

Boghaz' mouth fell open. "Mad," he whispered. "The poor fellow's lost his wits from shock."

Carse glanced inside. The guards were lounging out of earshot. They had no reason to care what went on on the balcony. There were three of them, mailed and armed. Boghaz was weaponless as a matter of course and Carse could not possibly escape unless he grew wings.

Swiftly the Earthman spoke.

"This venture of the Sea Kings is hopeless. The Dhuvians will help Sark and Khondor will be doomed. And that means you too, Boghaz. The Sarks will come and if you survive their attack, which is doubtful, they'll flay you alive and give what's left of you to the Dhuvians."

Boghaz thought about that and it was not a pleasant thought.

"But," he stammered, "to regain Rhiannon's weapons now—it's impossible. Even if you could escape from here no man alive could get into Sark and snatch them from under Garach's nose!"

"No man," said Carse. "But I'm not just a man, remember? And whose weapons were they to begin with?"

Realization began to dawn in the Valkisian's eyes. A great light broke over his moon face. He almost shouted and caught himself with Carse's hand already over his mouth.

"I salute you, Carse!" he whispered. "The Father of Lies himself could not do better." He was beside himself with ecstasy. "It is sublime. It is worthy of—of Boghaz!"

Then he sobered and shook his head. "But it is also sheer insanity."

Carse took him by the shoulders. "As it was before on the galley—nothing to lose, all to gain. Will you stand by me?"

The Valkisian closed his eyes. "I am tempted," he murmured. "As a craftsman, as an artist, I would like to see the flowering of this beautiful deceit."

He shivered all over. "Flayed alive, you say. And then the Dhuvians. I suppose you're right. We're dead men, anyway." His eyes popped open. "Hold on there! For Rhiannon all might be well in Sark but I'm only Boghaz, who mutinied against Ywain. Oh, no! I'm better off in Khondor."

"Stay, then, if you think so," Carse shook him. "You fat fool! I'll protect you. As Rhiannon I can do that. And as the saviours of Khondor, with those weapons in our hands, there's no end to what we can do. How would you like to be King of Valkis?"

"Well—" Boghaz sighed. "You would tempt the devil himself. And speaking of devils—" He looked narrowly at Carse. "Can you keep yours down? It's an uncanny thing to have a demon for a bunk-mate."

Carse said, "I can keep him down. You heard Rhiannon himself admit it."

"Then," said Boghaz, "we'd best move quickly before the Sea Kings end their council." He chuckled. "Old Ironbeard has helped us, ironically enough. Every man is ordered to duty and our crew is aboard the galley, waiting—and not very happy about it either!"

A moment later the guards in the inner room heard a piercing cry from Boghaz.

"Help! Come quickly—Carse has thrown himself into the sea!"

They rushed onto the balcony, where Boghaz was leaning out, pointing down to the churning waves below.

"I tried to hold him," he wailed, "but I could not."

One of the guards grunted. "Small loss," he said and then Carse stepped out of the shadows against the wall and struck him a sledgehammer blow that felled him, and Boghaz whirled around to lay a second man on his back.

The third one they knocked down between them before he could get his sword clear of the scabbard. The other two were climbing to their feet again with some idea of going on with the fight but Carse and the Valkisian had no time to waste and knew it. Fists hammered stunning blows with brutal accuracy and within a few minutes the three unconscious men were safely bound and gagged.

Carse started to take the sword from one of them, and Boghaz coughed with some embarrassment.

"Perhaps you'll want your own blade back," he said.

"Where is it?"

"Fortunately, just outside, where they made me leave it."

Carse nodded. It would be good to have the sword of Rhiannon in his hands again.

Crossing the room Carse stopped long enough to pick up a cloak belonging to one of the guards. He looked sidelong at Boghaz. "How did you so fortunately chance to have my sword?" he asked.

"Why, being your best friend and second in command, I claimed it." The Valkisian smiled tenderly. "You were about to die—and I knew you would want me to have it."

"Boghaz," said Carse, "your love for me is a beautiful thing."

"I have always been sentimental by nature." The Valkisian motioned him aside, at the door. "Let me go first."

He stepped out in the corridor, then nodded and Carse followed him. The long blade stood against the wall. He picked it up and smiled.

"From now on," he said, "remember, I am Rhiannon!"

There was little traffic in this part of the palace. The halls were dark, lighted at infrequent intervals by torches. Boghaz chuckled.

"I know my way around this place," he said. "In fact I have found ways in and out that even the Khonds have forgotten."

"Good," said Carse. "You lead then. We go first to find Ywain."

"*Ywain!*" Boghaz stared at him. "Are you crazy, Carse? This is no time to be toying with that vixen!"

Carse snarled. "She must be with us to bear witness in Sark that I am Rhiannon. Otherwise the whole scheme will fall. Now will you go?"

He had realized that Ywain was the keystone of his whole desperate gamble. His trump card was the fact that she had seen Rhiannon possess him.

"There is truth in what you say," Boghaz admitted, then added dismally, "But I like it not. First a devil, then a hellcat with poison on her claws—this is surely a voyage for madmen!"

Ywain was imprisoned on the same upper level. Boghaz led the way swiftly and they met no one. Presently, around the bend where two corridors met, Carse saw a single torch burning by a barred door that had one small opening in its upper half. A sleepy guard drowsed there over his spear.

Boghaz drew a long breath. "Ywain can convince the Sarks," he whispered, "but can you convince her?"

"I must," Carse answered grimly.

"Well then—I wish us luck!"

According to the plan they had made on the way Boghaz sauntered ahead to talk to the guard, who was glad to have news of what was going on. Then, in the middle of a sentence, Boghaz allowed his voice to trail off. Open-mouthed, he stared over the guard's shoulder.

The startled man swung around.

Carse came down the corridor. He strode as though he owned the world, the cloak thrown back from his shoulders, his tawny head erect, his eyes flashing. The wavering torchlight struck fire from his jewels and the sword of Rhiannon was a shaft of wicked silver in his hand.

He spoke in the ringing tones he remembered from the grotto.

"Down on your face, you scum of Khondor—unless you wish to die!"

The man stood transfixed, his spear half raised. Behind him Boghaz uttered a frightened whimper.

"By the gods," he moaned, "the devil has possessed him again. It is Rhiannon, broken free!"

Very godlike in the brazen light, Carse raised the sword, not as a weapon but as a talisman of power. He allowed himself to smile.

"So you know me. It is well." He bent his gaze on the white-faced guard. "Do *you* doubt, that I must teach you?"

"No," the guard answered hoarsely. "No, Lord!"

He went to his knees. The spear-point clashed on rock as he dropped it. Then he bellied down and hid his face in his hands.

Boghaz whimpered again, "Lord Rhiannon."

"Bind him," said Carse, "and open me this door."

It was done. Boghaz lifted the three heavy bars from their sockets. The door swung inward and Carse stood upon the threshold.

She was waiting, standing tensely erect in the gloom. They had not given her so much as a candle and the tiny cell was closed except for the barred slot in the door. The air was stale and dank with a taint of moldy straw from the pallet that was the only furniture. And she wore her fetters still.

Carse steeled himself. He wondered whether, in the hidden depths of his mind, the Cursed One watched. Almost, he thought, he heard the echo of dark laughter, mocking the man who played at being a god.

Ywain said, "Are you indeed Rhiannon?"

Marshal the deep proud voice, the look of brooding fire in the glance.

"You have known me before," said Carse. "How say you now?"

He waited, while her eyes searched him in the half light. And then slowly her head bent, stiffly as became Ywain of Sark even before Rhiannon.

"Lord," she said.

Carse laughed shortly and turned to the cringing Boghaz.

"Wrap her in the cloths from the pallet. You must carry her— and bear her gently, swine!"

Boghaz scurried to obey. Ywain was obviously furious at the indignity but she held her tongue on that score.

"We are escaping them?" she asked.

"We are leaving Khondor to its fate." Carse gripped the sword. "I would be in Sark when the Sea Kings come that I may blast them myself, with my own weapons!"

Boghaz covered her face with the rags. Her hauberk and the hampering chains were hidden. The Valkisian lifted what might have been only a dirty bundle to his massive shoulder. And over the bundle he gave Carse a beaming wink.

Carse himself was not so sure. In this moment, grasping at the chance for freedom, Ywain would not be too critical. But it was a long way to Sark.

Had he detected in her manner just the faintest note of mockery when she bent her head?

CHAPTER FIFTEEN
Under the Two Moons

BOGHAZ, WITH THE true instinct of his breed, had learned every rathole in Khondor. He took them out of the palace by a way so long disused that the dust lay inches thick and the postern door had almost rotted away. Then, by crumbling stairways and steep alleys that were no more than cracks in the rock, he led the way around the city.

Khondor seethed. The night wind carried echoes of hastening feet and taut voices. The upper air was full of beating wings where the Sky Folk went, dark against the stars.

There was no panic. But Carse could feel the anger of the city, and the hard grim tension of a people about to strike back against certain doom. From the distant temple he could hear the voices of women chanting to the gods.

The hurrying people they met paid them little heed. It was only a fat sailor with a bundle and a tall man muffled in a cloak, going down toward the harbor. What matter for notice in that?

They climbed the long, long steps downward to the basin and there was much coming and going on the dizzy way, but still they passed unchallenged. Each Khond was too full of his own worries this fateful night to pay attention to his neighbor.

Nevertheless Carse's heart was pounding and his ears ached from listening for the alarm which would surely come as soon as Ironbeard went up to slay his captive.

They gained the quays. Carse saw the tall mast of the galley towering above the longships and made for it with Boghaz panting at this heels.

Torches burned here by the hundreds. By their light fighting men and supplies were pouring aboard the longships. The rock walls rang with the tumult. Small craft darted between the outer moorings.

Carse kept his head lowered, shouldering his way through the crowd. The water was alive with Swimmers and there were women with set white faces who had come to bid their men farewell.

As they neared the galley Carse let Boghaz get ahead of him. He paused in the shelter of a pile of casks, pretending to bind up his sandal thong while the Valkisian went aboard with his burden. He heard the crew, sullen-faced and nervous, hailing Boghaz and asking for news.

Boghaz disposed of Ywain by dumping her casually in the cabin, and then called all hands forward for a conference by the wine butt, which was locked in the lazarette there. The Valkisian had his speech by heart.

"News?" Carse heard him say. "I'll give you news! Since Rold was taken there's an ugly temper in the city. We were their brothers yesterday. Today we're outlaws and enemies again. I've heard them talking in the wine shops and I tell you our lives aren't worth *that!*"

While the crew was muttering uneasily over that, Carse darted over the side unseen. Before he gained the cabin he heard Boghaz finish.

"There was a mob already gathering when I left. If we want to save our hides we'd better cast off now while we have the chance!"

Carse had been pretty sure what the reaction of the crew would be to that story and he was not sure at all that Boghaz was stretching it too much. He had seen mobs turn before and his crew of convict Sarks, Jekkarans and others might soon be in a nasty spot.

Now, with the cabin door closed and barred, he leaned against the panel, listening. He heard the padding of bare feet on the deck, the quick shouting of orders, the rattle of the blocks as the sails came down from the yards. The mooring lines were cast off. The sweeps came out with a ragged rumble. The galley rode free.

"Ironbeard's orders!" Boghaz shouted to someone on shore. "A mission for Khondor!"

The galley quivered, then began to gather way with the measured booming of the drum. And then, over all the near confusion of sound, Carse heard that his ears had been straining to hear—the distant roar from the crest of the rock, the alarm sweeping through the city, rushing toward the harbor stair.

He stood in an agony of fear lest everyone else should hear it too and know its meaning without being told. But the din of the harbor covered it long enough and by the time word had been brought down from the crest the black galley was already in the road stead, speeding down into the mouth of the fiord.

In the darkness of the cabin Ywain spoke quietly. "Lord Rhiannon—may I be allowed to breathe?"

He knelt and stripped the cloths from her and she sat up.

"My thanks. Well, we are free of the palace and the harbor but there still remains the fiord. I heard the outcry."

"Aye," said Carse. "And the Sky Folk will carry word ahead." He laughed. "Let us see if they can stop Rhiannon by flinging pebbles from the cliffs!"

He left her then, ordering her to remain where she was, and went out on deck.

They were well along the channel now, racing under a fast stroke. The sails were beginning to catch the wind that blew between the cliffs. He tried to remember how the ballista defenses were set, counting on the fact that they were meant to bear on ships coming into the fiord, not going out.

Speed would be the main thing. If they could drive the galley fast enough they'd have a chance.

In the faint light of Deimos no one saw him. Not until Phobos topped the cliffs and sent a shaft of greenish light. Then the men saw him there, his cloak whipping in the wind, the long sword in his hands.

A strange sort of cry went up—half welcome for the Carse they remembered, half fear because of what they had heard about him in Khondor.

He didn't give them time to think. Swinging the sword high, he roared at them, "Pull, there, you apes! Pull, or they'll sink us!"

Man or devil, they knew he spoke the truth. They pulled.

Carse leaped up to the steersman's platform. Boghaz was already there. He cowered convincingly against the rail as Carse approached but the man at the tiller regarded him with wolfish eyes in which there was an ugly spark. It was the man with the branded cheek, who had been at the oar with Jaxart on the day of the mutiny.

"I'm captain now," he said to Carse. "I'll not have you on my ship to curse it!"

Carse said with terrible slowness, "I see you do not know me. Tell him, man of Valkis!"

But there was no need for Boghaz to speak. There came a whistling of pinions down the wind and a winged man stooped low in the moonlight over the ship.

"Turn back! Turn back!" he cried. "You bear—*Rhiannon!*"

"Aye!" Carse shouted back. "Rhiannon's wrath, Rhiannon's power!"

He lifted the sword hilt high so that the dark jewel blazed evilly in Phobos' light.

"Will you stand against me? Will you dare?"

The Skyman swerved away and rose wailing in the wind. Carse turned upon the steersman.

"And you," he said. "How say you now?"

He saw the wolf-eyes flicker from the blazing jewel to his own face and back again. The look of terror he was beginning to know too well came into them and they dropped.

"I dare not stand against Rhiannon," the man said hoarsely.

"Give me the helm," said Carse, and the other stood aside, the brand showing livid on his whitened cheek.

"Make speed," Carse ordered, "if you would live."

And speed they made, so that the galley went with a frightening rush between the cliffs, a black and ghostly ship between the white fire of the fiord and the cold green moonlight. Carse saw the open sea ahead and steeled himself, praying.

A whining snarl echoed from the rock as the first of the great ballistas crashed. A spout of water rose by the galley's bow and she shuddered and raced on.

Crouched over the tiller bar, his cloak streaming, his face intense and strange in the eery glow, Carse ran the gauntlet in the throat of the fiord.

Ballistas twanged and thundered. Great stones rained into the water, so that they sailed through a burning cloud of mist and spray. But it was as Carse had hoped. The defenses, invincible to frontal attack, were weak when taken in reverse. The bracketing of the channel was imperfect, the aim poor against a fleeting target. Those things and the headlong speed of the galley saved them.

They came out into open water. The last stone fell far astern and they were free. There would be quick pursuit—that he knew. But for the moment they were safe.

Carse realized then the difficulties of being a god. He wanted to sit down on the deck and take a long pull at the wine cask to get over his shakes. But instead he had to force a ringing laugh, as though it amused him to see these childish humans try to prevail against the invincible.

"Here, you who call yourself captain! Take the helm—and set a course for Sark."

"Sark!" The unlucky man had much to contend with that night. "My Lord Rhiannon, have pity! We are proscribed convicts in Sark!"

"Rhiannon will protect you," Boghaz said.

"*Silence!*" roared Carse. "Who are you to speak for Rhiannon?" Boghaz cringed abjectly and Carse said, "Fetch the Lady Ywain to me—but first strike off her chains."

He descended the ladder to stand upon the deck, waiting. Behind him he heard the branded man groan and mutter, "*Ywain!* Gods above, the Khonds would have been a better death!"

Carse stood unmoving and the men watched him, not daring to speak, wanting to rise and kill him, but afraid. Afraid of the unknown, shivering at the power of the Cursed One that could blast them all.

Ywain came to him, free of her chains now, and bowed. He turned and called out to the crew.

"You rose against her once, following the barbarian. Now the barbarian is no more as you knew him. And you will serve Ywain again. Serve her well and she will forget your crime."

He saw her eyes blaze at that. She started to protest and he gave her a look that stopped the words in her throat.

"Pledge them," he commanded. "On the honor of Sark."

She obeyed. But it seemed to Carse again that she was still not quite convinced that he was actually Rhiannon.

She followed him to the cabin and asked if she might enter. He gave her leave and sent Boghaz after wine and then for a time there was silence. Carse sat brooding in Ywain's chair, trying to still the nervous pounding of his heart and she watched him from under lowered lids.

The wine was brought. Boghaz hesitated and then perforce left them alone.

"Sit down," said Carse, "and drink."

Ywain pulled up a low stool and sat with her long legs thrust out before her, slender as a boy in her black mail. She drank and said nothing.

Carse said abruptly, "You doubt me still."

She started, "No, Lord!"

Carse laughed. "Don't think to lie to me. A still-necked, haughty wench you are, Ywain, and clever. An excellent prince for Sark despite your sex."

Her mouth twisted rather bitterly. "My father Garach fashioned me as I am. A weakling with no son—someone had to carry the sword while he toyed with the scepter."

"I think," said Carse, "that you have not altogether hated it."

She smiled. "No. I was never bred for silken cushions." She continued suddenly, "But let us have no more talk of my doubting, Lord Rhiannon. I have known you before—once in this cabin when you faced S'San and again in the place of the Wise Ones. I know you now."

"It does not greatly matter whether you doubt or not, Ywain. The barbarian alone overcame you and I think Rhiannon would have no trouble."

She flushed an angry red. Her lingering suspicion of him was plain now—her anger with him betrayed it.

"The barbarian did not overcome me! He kissed me and I let him enjoy that kiss so that I could leave the mark of it on his face forever!"

Carse nodded, goading her. "And for a moment you enjoyed it also. You're a woman, Ywain, for all your short tunic and your mail. And a woman always knows the one man who can master her."

"You think so?" she whispered.

She had come close to him now, her red lips parted as they had been before—tempting, deliberately provocative.

"I know it," he said.

"If you were merely the barbarian and nothing else," she murmured, "I might know it also."

The trap was almost undisguised. Carse waited until the tense silence had gone flat. Then he said coldly, "Very likely you would. However I am not the barbarian now, but Rhiannon. And it is time you slept."

He watched her with grim amusement as she drew away, disconcerted and perhaps for the first time in her life completely at a loss. He knew that he had dispelled her lingering doubt about him for the time being at least.

He said, "You may have the inner cabin."

"Yes, Lord," she answered and now there was no mockery in her tone.

She turned and crossed the cabin slowly. She pushed open the inner door and then halted, her hand on the doorpost, and he saw an expression of loathing come into her face.

"Why do you hesitate?" he asked.

"The place still reeks of the serpent taint," she said. "I had rather sleep on deck."

"Those are strange words, Ywain. S'San was your counselor, your friend. I was forced to slay him to save the barbarian's life— but surely Ywain of Sark has no dislike of her allies!"

"Not my allies—Garach's." She turned and faced him and he saw that her anger over her discomfiture had made her forget caution.

"Rhiannon or no Rhiannon," she cried, "I will say what has been in my mind to say all these years. I hate your crawling pupils of Caer Dhu! I loathe them utterly—and now you may slay me if you will!"

And she strode out onto the deck, letting the door slam shut behind her.

Carse sat still behind the table. He was trembling all over with nervous strain and presently he would pour wine to aid him. But just now he was amazed to find how happy it could make him to know that Ywain too hated Caer Dhu.

The wind had dropped by midnight and for hours the galley forged on under oars, moving at far less than her normal speed because they were short-handed in the rowers' pit, having lost the Khonds that made up the full number.

And at dawn the lookout sighted four tiny specks on the horizon that were the hulls of longships, coming on from Khondor.

CHAPTER SIXTEEN
Voice of the Serpent

CARSE STOOD ON the afterdeck with Boghaz. It was mid-morning. The calm still held and now the longships were close enough to be seen from the deck.

Boghaz said, "At this rate they'll overhaul us by nightfall."

"Yes." Carse was worried. Under-manned as she was the galley could not hope to outdistance the Khonds under oars alone. And the last thing Carse wanted was to be forced into the position of fighting Ironbeard's men. He knew he couldn't do it.

"They'll break their hearts to catch us," he said. "And these are only the van. The whole of the Sea Kings' fleet will be coming on behind them."

Boghaz looked at the following ships. "Do you think we'll ever reach Sark?"

"Not unless we raise a fair wind," Carse said grimly, "and even then not by much of a margin. Do you know any prayers?"

"I was instructed in my youth," answered Boghaz piously.

"Then pray!"

But all that long hot day there was no more than a breath of air to ripple the galley's sails. The men wearied at the sweeps. They had not much heart for the business at best, being trapped between two evils with a demon for captain, and they had only so much strength.

The longships doggedly, steadily, grew closer.

In the late afternoon, when the setting sun made a magnifying glass of the lower air the lookout reported other ships far back in the distance. Many ships—the armada of the Sea Kings.

Carse looked up into the empty sky, bitter of heart.

The breeze began to strengthen. As the sails filled the rowers roused themselves and pulled with renewed vigor. Presently Carse ordered the sweeps in. The wind blew strongly. The galley picked up speed and the longships could no more than hold their own.

Carse knew the galley's speed. She was a fast sailor and with her great spread of canvas might hope to keep well ahead of the pursuers if the wind held.

If the wind held . . .

The next few days were enough to drive a man mad. Carse drove the men in the pit without mercy and each time the sweeps had to be run out the beat grew slower as they reached the point of exhaustion.

By the narrowest margin Carse kept the galley ahead. Once, when it seemed they were surely caught, a sudden storm saved them by scattering the lighter ships, but they came on again. And now a man could see the horizon dotted with a host of sails, where the armada irresistibly advanced.

The immediate pursuers grew from four to five, and then to seven. Carse remembered the old adage that a stern chase is a long one but it seemed that this one could not go on much longer.

There came another time of flat hot calm. The rowers drooped and sweated at the oars driven only by their fear of the Khonds and try as they would there was no bite in the stroke.

Carse stood by the after rail, watching, his face lined and grim. The game was up. The lean longships were putting on a burst of speed, closing in for the kill.

Suddenly, sharply, there came a hail from the masthead.

"Sail ho!"

Carse whirled, following the line of the lookout's pointing arm.

"Sark ships!"

He saw them ahead, racing up under a fast beat, three tall war-galleys of the patrol. Leaping to the edge of the rowers' pit, he shouted to the men.

"Pull, you dogs! Lay into it! There's help on the way!"

They found their last reserves of energy. The galley made a desperate lurching run. Ywain came to Carse's side.

"We're close to Sark now, Lord Rhiannon. If we can keep ahead a little longer . . ."

The Khonds rushed down on them, pushing furiously in a last attempt to ram and sink the galley before the Sarks could reach them. But they were too late.

The patrol ships swept by. They charged in among the Khonds and scattered them and the air was filled with shouts and the twanging of bowstrings, and the terrible ripping sounds of splintering oars as a whole bank was crushed into matchwood.

There began a running fight that lasted all afternoon. The desperate Khonds hung on and would not be driven off. The Sark ships closed in around the galley, a mobile wall of defense. Time and again the Khonds attacked, their light swift craft darting in hornet-like, and were driven off. The Sarks carried ballistas, and Carse saw two of the Khond ships holed and sunk by the hurtling stones.

A light breeze began to blow. The galley picked up speed. And now blazing arrows flew, searching out the bellying sails. Two of the escort ships fell back with their canvas ablaze but the Khonds suffered also. There were only three of them left in the fight and the galley was by now well ahead of them.

They came in sight of the Sark coast, a low dark line above the water. And then, to Carse's great relief, other ships came out to meet them, drawn by the fighting, and the three remaining Khond longships put about and drew off.

It was all easy after that. Ywain was in her own place again. Fresh rowers were put aboard from other ships and one swift craft went ahead of them to carry warning of the attack and news of Ywain's coming.

But the smoke of the burning longships astern was a painful thing to Carse. He looked at the massed sails of the Sea Kings in the far distance and felt the huge and crushing weight of the battle that was to come. It seemed to him in that moment that there was no hope.

They came in late afternoon into the harbor of Sark. A broad estuary offered anchorage for countless ships and on both sides of the channel the city sprawled in careless strength.

It was a city whose massive arrogance suited the men who had built it. Carse saw great temples and the squat magnificence of the palace, crowning the highest hill. The buildings were almost ugly in their solid strength, their buttressed shoulders jutting against the sky, brilliant with harsh colors and strong designs.

Already this whole harbor area was in a feverish sweat of activity. Word of the Sea Kings' coming had started a swift manning of ships and readying of defenses, the uproar and tumult of a city preparing for war.

Boghaz, beside him, muttered, "We're mad to walk like this into the dragon's throat. If you can't carry it off as Rhiannon, if you make one slip . . ."

Carse said, "I can do it. I've had considerable practice by now in playing the Cursed One."

But inwardly he was shaken. Confronted by the massive might of Sark it seemed a mad insolence to attempt to play the god here.

Crowds along the waterfront cheered Ywain wildly as she disembarked. And they stared in some amazement at the tall man with her, who looked like a Khond and wore a great sword.

Soldiers formed a guard around them and forced a way through the excited mob. The cheering followed them as they went up through the crowded city streets toward the brooding palace.

They passed at length into the cool dimness of the palace halls. Carse strode down huge echoing rooms with inlaid floors and massive pillars that supported giant beams covered with gold. He noticed that the serpent motif was strong in the decorations.

He wished he had Boghaz with him. He had been forced, for appearance sake, to leave the fat thief behind and he felt terribly alone.

At the silvery doors of the throne room the guard halted. A chamberlain wearing mail under his velvet gown came forward to greet Ywain.

"Your father, the Sovereign King Garach, is overjoyed at your safe return and wishes to welcome you. But he begs you to wait as he is closeted with the Lord Hishah, the emissary from Caer Dhu."

Ywain's lips twisted. "So already he asks aid of the Serpent." She nodded imperiously at the closed door. "Tell the king I will see him now."

The chamberlain protested. "But, Highness—"

"Tell him," said Ywain, "or I will enter without permission. Say that there is one with me who demands admittance and whom not even Garach nor all Caer Dhu may deny."

The chamberlain looked in frank puzzlement at Carse. He hesitated, then bowed and went in through the silver doors.

Carse had caught the note of bitterness in Ywain's voice when she spoke of the Serpent. He taxed her with it.

"No, Lord," she said. "I spoke once and you were lenient. It is not my place to speak again. Besides"—she shrugged—"you see how my father bars me from his confidence in this, even though I must fight his battles for him."

"You do not wish aid from Caer Dhu even now?"

She remained silent, and Carse said, "I bid you to speak!"

"Very well then. It is natural for two strong peoples to fight for mastery when their interests clash on every shore of the same sea. It is natural for men to want power. I could have gloried in this coming battle, gloried in victory over Khondor. But—"

"Go on."

She cried out then with controlled passion. "But I have wished that Sark had grown great by fair force of arms, man against man, as it was in the old days before Garach made alliance with Caer Dhu! And now there is no glory in a victory won before even the hosts have met."

"And your people," asked Carse. "Do they share your feelings in this?"

"They do, Lord. But enough are tempted by power and spoils—"

She broke off, looking Carse straight in the face.

"I have already said enough to bring your wrath upon me. Therefore I will finish, for I think now that Sark is truly doomed, even in victory. The Serpent gives us aid not for our sakes, but as part of its own design. We have become no more than tools by which Caer Dhu gains its end. And now that you have come back to lead the Dhuvians—"

She stopped and there was no need for her to finish. The opening of the door saved Carse from the necessity of an answer.

The chamberlain said apologetically, "Highness, your father sends answer that he does not understand your bold words and again begs you to wait his pleasure."

Ywain thrust him angrily aside and strode to the tall doors, flinging them open. She stood back and said to Carse, "Lord, will you enter?"

He drew a deep breath and entered, striding down the long dim length of the throne room like a very god, with Ywain following behind.

The place seemed empty except for Garach, who had sprung to his feet on the dais at the far end. He wore a robe of black velvet worked in gold and he had Ywain's graceful height and handsomeness of feature. But her honest strength was not in him, nor her pride, nor her level glance. For all his graying beard he had a mouth of a petulant greedy child.

Beside him, withdrawn into the shadows by the high seat, another stood also. A dark figure, hooded and cloaked, its face concealed, its hands hidden in the wide sleeves of its robe.

"What means this?" cried Garach angrily. "Daughter or not, Ywain, I'll not stand for such insolence!"

Ywain bent her knee. "My father," she said clearly, "I bring you the Lord Rhiannon of the Quiru, returned from the dead."

Garach's face paled by degrees to the color of ash. His mouth opened, but no words came. He stared at Carse and then at Ywain and finally at the cowled, hooded Dhuvian.

"This is madness," he stammered at last.

"Nevertheless," said Ywain, "I bear witness to its truth. Rhiannon's mind lives in the body of the barbarian. He spoke to the Wise Ones at Khondor and he has spoken since to me. It is Rhiannon who stands before you."

Again there was silence as Garach stared and stared and trembled. Carse stood tall and lordly, outwardly contemptuous of doubt and waiting for acknowledgement.

But the old chilling fear was in him. He knew that ophidian eyes watched him from the shadow under the Dhuvian's cowl and it seemed that he could feel their cold gaze sliding through his imposture as a knife blade slips through paper.

The mind-knowledge of the Halflings. The strong extra-sensory perception that could see beyond the appearances of the flesh. And the Dhuvians, for all their evil, were Halflings too.

Carse wanted nothing more at that moment than to break and run. But he forced himself to play the god, arrogant and self-assured, smiling at Garach's fear.

Deep within his brain, in the corner that was no longer his own, he felt a strange and utter stillness. It was as though the invader, the Cursed One, had gone.

Carse forced himself to speak, making his voice ring back from the walls in stern echoes.

"The memories of children are indeed short when even the favorite pupil has forgotten the master."

And he bent his gaze upon Hishah the Dhuvian.

"Do you also doubt me, child of the snake? Must I teach you again, as I taught S'San?"

He lifted the great sword and Garach's eyes flickered to Ywain. She said, "The Lord Rhiannon slew S'San, aboard the galley."

Garach dropped to his knees.

"Lord," he said submissively, "what is your will?"

Carse ignored him, looking still at the Dhuvian. And the cowled figure moved forward with a peculiar gliding step and spoke in its soft hateful voice.

"Lord, I also ask—what is your will?"

The dark robe rippled as the creature seemed to kneel.

"It is well." Carse crossed his hands over the hilt of the sword, dimming the lustre of the jewel.

"The fleet of the Sea Kings stand in to attack soon. I would have my ancient weapons brought to me that I may crush the enemies of Sark and Caer Dhu, who are also my enemies."

A great hope sprang into Garach's eyes. It was obvious that fear gnawed his vitals—fear of many things, Carse thought, but just now, above all, fear of the Sea Kings. He glanced aside at Hishah and the cowled creature said, "Lord, your weapons have been taken to Caer Dhu."

The Earthman's heart sank. Then he remembered Rold of Khondor, and how they must have broken him to get the secret of the Tomb and a blind rage came over him. The snarl of fury in his voice was not feigned, only the sense of his words.

"You dared to tamper with the power of Rhiannon?" He advanced toward the Dhuvian. "Can it be that the pupil now hopes to outrival the master?"

"No, Lord." The veiled head bowed. "We have but kept your weapons safe for you."

Carse permitted his features to relax somewhat.

"Very well, then. See that they are returned to me here and at once!"

Hishah rose. "Yes, Lord. I will go now to Caer Dhu to do your bidding."

The Dhuvian glided toward an inner door and was gone, leaving Carse in a secret sweat of mingled relief and apprehension.

CHAPTER SEVENTEEN
Caer Dhu

THE NEXT FEW hours were an eternity of unbearable tension for Carse.

He demanded an apartment for himself, on the ground that he must have privacy to draw his plans. And there he paced up and down in a fine state of nerves, looking most ungodlike.

It seemed that he had succeeded. The Dhuvian had accepted him. Perhaps, he thought, the Serpent folk after all lacked the astoundingly developed extra-sensory powers of the Swimmers and the winged men.

It appeared that all he had to do now was to wait for the Dhuvian to return with the weapons, load them aboard his ship and go away. He could do that, for no one would dare to question the plans of Rhiannon and he had time also. The Sea Kings' fleet was standing off, waiting for all its force to come up. There would be no attack before dawn, none at all if he succeeded.

But some raw primitive nerve twitched to the sense of danger and Carse was oppressed by a foreboding fear.

He sent for Boghaz on the pretext of giving orders concerning the galley. His real reason was that he could not bear to be alone. The fat thief was jubilant when he heard the news.

"You have brought it off," he chuckled, rubbing his hands together in delight. "I have always said, Carse, that sheer gall would carry a man through anything. I, Boghaz, could not have done better."

Carse said dourly, "I hope you're right."

Boghaz gave him a sidelong glance. "Carse—"

"Yes?"

"What of the Cursed One himself?"

"Nothing. Not a sign. It worries me, Boghaz. I have the feeling that he's waiting."

"When you get the weapons in your hands," Boghaz said meaningly, "I'll stand by you with a belaying pin."

The soft-footed chamberlain brought word at last that Hishah had returned from Caer Dhu and awaited audience with him.

"It is well," said Carse and then nodded curtly toward Boghaz. "This man will come with me to supervise the handling of the weapons."

The Valkisian's ruddy cheeks lost several shades of color but he came perforce at Carse's heels.

Garach and Ywain were in the throne room and the black-cowled creature from Caer Dhu. All bowed as Carse entered.

"Well," he demanded of the Dhuvian, "have you obeyed my command?"

"Lord," said Hishah softly, "I took counsel with the Elders, who send you this word. Had they known that the Lord Rhiannon had returned they would not have presumed to touch those things which are his. And now they fear to touch them again lest in their ignorance they do damage or cause destruction."

"Therefore, Lord, they beg you to arrange this matter yourself. Also they have not forgotten their love for Rhiannon, whose teachings raised them from the dust. They wish to welcome you to your old kingdom in Caer Dhu, for your children have been long in darkness and would once again know the light of Rhiannon's wisdom, and his strength."

Hishah made a low obeisance. "Lord, will you grant them this?"

Carse stood silent for a moment, trying desperately to conceal his dread. He could not go to Caer Dhu. He dared not go! How long could he hope to conceal his deception from the children of the Serpent, the oldest deceiver of all?

If, indeed, he had concealed it at all. Hishah's soft words reeked of a subtle trap.

And trapped he was and knew it. He dared not go—but even more he dared not refuse.

He said, "I am pleased to grant them their request."

Hishah bowed his head in thanks. "All preparations are made. King Garach and his daughter will accompany you that you may be suitably attended. Your children realize the need for haste—the barge is waiting."

"Good." Carse turned on his heel, fixing Boghaz as he did so with a steely look.

"You will attend me also, man of Valkis. I may have need of you with regard to the weapons."

Boghaz got his meaning. If he had paled before he turned now a livid white with pure horror but there was not a word he could say. Like a man led to execution he followed Carse out of the throne room.

Night brooded black and heavy as they embarked at the palace stair in a low black craft without sail or oar. Creatures hooded and robed like Hishah thrust long poles into the water and the barged moved out into the estuary, heading up away from the sea.

Garach crouched amid the sable cushions of a divan, an unkingly figure with shaking hands and cheeks the color of bone. His eyes kept furtively seeking the muffled form of Hishah. It was plain that he did not relish this visit to the court of his allies.

Ywain had withdrawn herself to the far side of the barge, where she sat looking out into the somber darkness of the marshy shore. Carse thought she seemed more depressed than she ever had when she was a prisoner in chains.

He too sat by himself, outwardly lordly and magnificent, inwardly shaken to the soul. Boghaz crouched nearby. His eyes were the eyes of a sick man.

And the Cursed One, the real Rhiannon, was still. Too still. In that buried corner of Carse's mind there was not a stir, not a flicker. It seemed that the dark outcast of the Quiru was like all the others aboard, withdrawn and waiting.

It seemed a long way up the estuary. The water slid past the barge with a whisper of sibilant mirth. The black-robed figures bent and swayed at the poles. Now and again a bird cried from the marshland and the night air was heavy and brooding.

Then, in the light of the little low moons, Carse saw ahead the ragged walls and ramparts of a city rising from the mists, an old,

old city walled like a castle. It sprawled away into ruin on all sides and only the great central keep was whole.

There was a flickering radiance in the air around the place. Carse thought that it was his imagination, a visual illusion caused by the moonlight and the glowing water and the pale mist.

The barge drew in toward a crumbling quay. It came to rest and Hishah stepped ashore, bowing as he waited for Rhiannon to pass.

Carse strode up along the quay with Garach and Ywain and the shivering Boghaz following. Hishah remained deferentially at the Earthman's heels.

A causeway of black stone, much cracked by the weight of years, led up toward the citadel. Carse set his feet resolutely upon it. Now he was sure that he could see a faint, pulsing web of light around Caer Dhu. It lay over the whole city, glimmering with a steely luminescence, like starlight on a frosty night.

He did not like the look of it. As he approached it, where it crossed the causeway like a veil before the great gate, he liked it less and less.

Yet no one spoke, no one faltered. He seemed to be expected the lead the way, and he did not dare to betray his ignorance of the nature of the thing. So he forced his steps to go on, strong and sure.

He was close enough to the gleaming web to feel a strange prickling of force. One more stride would have taken him into it. And then Hishah said sharply in his ear, "Lord! Have you forgotten the Veil, whose touch is death?"

Carse recoiled. A shock of fear went through him and at the same time he realized that he had blundered badly.

He said quickly, "Of course I have not forgotten!"

"No, Lord," Hishah murmured. "How indeed could you forget when it was you who taught us the secret of the Veil which warps space and shields Caer Dhu from any force?"

Carse knew now that that gleaming web was a defensive barrier of energy, of such potent energy that it somehow set up a space-strain which nothing could penetrate.

It seemed incredible. Yet Quiru science had been great and Rhiannon had taught some of it to the forefathers of these Dhuvians.

"How, indeed, could *you* forget?" Hishah repeated.

There was no hint of mockery in his words and yet Carse felt it was there.

The Dhuvian stepped forward, raising his sleeved arms in a signal to some watcher within the gate. The luminescence of the Veil died out above the causeway, leaving a path open through it.

And as Carse turned to go on he saw that Ywain was staring at him with a look of startled wonder in which a doubt was already beginning to grow. The great gate swung open and the Lord Rhiannon of the Quiru was received into Caer Dhu.

The ancient halls were dimly lighted by what seemed to be globes of prisoned fire that stood on tripods at long intervals, shedding a cool greenish glow. The air was warm and the taint of the Serpent lay heavy in it, closing Carse's throat with its hateful sickliness.

Hishah went before them now and that in itself was a sign of danger, since Rhiannon should have known the way. But Hishah said that he wished the honor of announcing his lord and Carse could do nothing but choke down his growing terror and follow.

They came into a vast central place, closed in by towering walls of the black rock that rose to a high vault, lost in darkness overhead. Below, a single large globe lightened the heavy shadows.

Little light for human eyes. But even that was too much!

For here the children of the serpent were gathered to greet their lord. And here in their own place they were not shrouded in the cowled robes they wore when they went among men.

The Swimmers belonged to the sea, the Sky folk to the high air, and they were perfect and beautiful in accordance with their elements. Now Carse saw the third pseudo-human race of the Halflings—the children of the hidden places, the perfect, dreadfully perfect offspring of another great order of life.

In the first overwhelming shock of revulsion Carse was hardly aware of Hishah's voice saying the name of Rhiannon and the soft, sibilant cry of greeting that followed was only the tongue of nightmare speaking.

From the edges of the wide floor they hailed him and from the open galleries above, their depthless eyes glittering, their narrow ophidian heads bowed in homage.

Sinuous bodies that moved with effortless ease, seeming to flow rather than step. Hands with supple jointless fingers and feet that made no sound and lipless mouths that seemed to open always on silent laughter, infinitely cruel. And all through that vast place whispered a dry harsh rustling, the light friction of skin that had lost its primary scales but not its serpentine roughness.

Carse raised the sword of Rhiannon in acknowledgement of that welcome and forced himself to speak.

"Rhiannon is pleased by the greeting of his children."

It seemed to him that a little hissing ripple of mirth ran through the great hall. But he could not be sure, and Hishah said,

"My Lord, here are your ancient weapons."

They were in the center of the cleared space. All the cryptic mechanisms he had seen in the Tomb were here, the great flat crystal wheel, the squat looped metal rods, the others, all glittering in the dim light.

Carse's heart leaped and settled to a heavy pounding. "Good," he said. "The time is short—take them aboard the barge, that I may return to Sark at once."

"Certainly, Lord," said Hishah. "But will you not inspect them first to make sure that all is well. Our ignorant handling . . ."

Carse strode to the weapons and made a show of examining them. Then he nodded.

"No damage has been done. And now—"

Hishah broke in, unctuously courteous. "Before you go, will you not explain the workings of these instruments? Your children were always hungry for knowledge."

"There is no time for that," Carse said angrily. "Also, you are as you say—children. You could not comprehend."

"Can it be, Lord," asked Hishah very softly, "that you yourself do not comprehend?"

There was a moment of utter stillness. The icy certainty of doom took Carse in its grip. He saw now that the ranks of the Dhuvians had closed in behind him, barring all hope of escape.

Within the circle Garach and Ywain and Boghaz stood with him. There was shocked amazement on Garach's face and the Valkisian sagged with the weight of horror that had come as no surprise to him. Ywain alone was not amazed, or horrified. She looked at Carse with the eyes of a woman who fears but in a different way. It came to Carse that she feared for him, that she did not want him to die.

In a last desperate attempt to save himself Carse cried out furiously.

"What means this insolence? Would you have me take up my weapons and use them against you?"

"Do so, if you can," Hishah said softly. "Do so, oh false Rhiannon, for assuredly by no other means will you ever leave Caer Dhu!"

CHAPTER EIGHTEEN
The Wrath of Rhiannon

CARSE STOOD WHERE he was, surrounded by the crystal and metal mechanisms that had no meaning for him, and knew with terrible finality that he was beaten. And now the hissing laughter broke forth on all sides, infinitely cruel and jeering.

Garach put out a trembling hand toward Hishah. "Then," he stammered, "this is not Rhiannon?"

"Even your human mind should tell you that much now," answered Hishah contemptuously. He had thrown back his cowl and now he moved toward Carse, his ophidian eyes full of mockery.

"By the touching of minds alone I would have known you false but even that I did not need. You, Rhiannon! Rhiannon of the Quiru, who came in peace and brotherhood to greet his children in Caer Dhu!"

The stealthy evil laughter hissed from every Dhuvian throat and Hishah threw his head back, the skin of his throat pulsing with his mirth.

"Look at him, my brothers! Hail Rhiannon, who did not know of the Veil nor why it guards Caer Dhu!"

And they hailed him, bowing low.

Carse stood very still. For the moment he had even forgotten to be afraid.

"You fool," said Hishah. "Rhiannon hated us at the end. For at the end he learned his folly, learned that the pupils to whom he gave the crumbs of knowledge had grown too clever. With the Veil, whose secret he had taught us, we made our city impregnable even to his mighty weapons, so that when he turned finally against us it was too late."

Carse said slowly, "Why did he turn against you?"

Hishah laughed. "He learned the use we had for the knowledge he had given us."

Ywain came forward, one step, and said, "What was that use?"

"I think you know already," Hishah answered. "That is why you and Garach were summoned here—not only to see this imposter unmasked but to learn once and for all your place in our world."

His soft voice had in it now the bite of the conqueror.

"Since Rhiannon was locked in his tomb we have gained subtle dominance on every shore of the White Sea. We are few in number and averse to open warfare. Therefore we have worked through the human kingdoms, using your greedy people as our tools."

"Now we have the weapons of Rhiannon. Soon we will master their use and then we will no longer need human tools. The Children of the Serpent will rule in every palace—and we will require only obedience and respect from our subjects."

"How think you of that, Ywain of the proud head, who have always loathed and scorned us?"

"I think," said Ywain, "that I will fall upon my own sword first."

Hishah shrugged. "Fall then." He turned to Garach. "And you?"

But Garach had already crumpled to the stones in a dead faint.

Hishah turned again to Carse. "And now," he said, "you shall see how we welcome our lord!"

Boghaz moaned and covered his face with his hands. Carse gripped the futile sword tighter and asked in a strange, low voice,

"And no one ever knew that Rhiannon had finally turned against you Dhuvians?"

Hishah answered softly, "The Quiru knew but nevertheless they condemned Rhiannon because his repentance came too late. Other than they only we knew. And why should we tell the world when it pleased our humor to see Rhiannon, who hated us, cursed as our friend?"

Carse closed his eyes. The world rocked under him, and there was a roaring in his ears, as the revelation burst upon him.

Rhiannon had spoken the truth in the place of the Wise Ones. Had spoken truth when he voiced his hatred of the Dhuvians!

The hall was filled with a sound like the rustling of dry leaves as the ranks of the Dhuvians closed gently in toward Carse.

With an effort of will almost beyond human strength Carse threw open all the channels of his mind, trying desperately now in this last minute to reach inward to that strangely silent, hidden corner.

He cried aloud, *"Rhiannon!"*

That hoarse cry made the Dhuvians pause. Not because of fear but because of laughter. This, indeed, was the climax of the jest!

Hishah cried, "Aye, call upon Rhiannon! Perhaps he will come from his Tomb to aid you!"

And they watched Carse out of their depthless jeering eyes as he swayed in torment.

But Ywain knew. Swiftly she moved to Carse's side and her sword came rasping out of the sheath, to protect him as long as it could.

Hishah laughed. "A fitting pair—the princess without an empire and the would-be-god!"

Carse said again, in a broken whisper, *"Rhiannon!"*

And Rhiannon answered.

From the depths of Carse's mind where he had lain hidden the Cursed One came, surging in terrible strength through every cell and atom of the Earthman's brain, possessing him utterly now that Carse had opened the way.

As it had been before in the place of the Wise Ones the consciousness of Matthew Carse stood aside in his own body and watched and listened.

He heard the voice of Rhiannon—the real and godlike voice that he had only copied—ring forth from his own lips in anger that was beyond human power to know.

"Behold your Lord, oh crawling children of the Serpent! Behold— and die!"

The mocking laughter died away into silence. Hishah gave back and into his eyes came the beginning of fear.

Rhiannon's voice rolled out, thundering against the walls. The strength and fury of Rhiannon blazed in the Earthman's face and now his body seemed to tower over the Dhuvians and the sword was a thing of lightning in his hands.

"What now of the touching of minds, Hishah? Probe deeply—more deeply than you did before when your feeble power could not penetrate the mental barrier I set up against you!"

Hishah voiced a high and hissing scream. He recoiled in horror and the circle of the Dhuvians broke as they turned to seek their weapons, their lipless mouths stretched wide in fear.

Rhiannon laughed, the terrible laughter of one who has waited through an age for vengeance and finds it at last.

"Run! Run and strive—for in your great wisdom you have let Rhiannon through your guarding Veil and death is on Caer Dhu!"

And the Dhuvians ran, writhing in the shadows as they caught up the weapons they had not thought to need. The green light glinted on the shining tubes and prisms.

But the hand of Carse, guided now by the sure knowledge of Rhiannon, had darted toward the biggest of the ancient weapons—toward the rim of the great flat crystal wheel. He set the wheel to spinning.

There must have been some intricate triggering of power within the metal globe, some hidden control that his fingers touched. Carse never knew. He only knew that a strange dark halo appeared in the dim air, enclosing himself and Ywain and the shuddering Boghaz and Garach, who had risen doglike to his hands and knees and was watching with eyes that held no shred of sanity. The ancient weapons were also enclosed in that ring of dark force, and a faint singing rose from the crystal rods.

The dark ring began to expand, like a circular wave sweeping outward.

The weapons of the Dhuvians strove against it. Lances of lightning, of cold flame and searing brilliance, leaped toward it, struck—and splintered and died. Powerful electric discharges that broke themselves on the invisible dielectric that shielded Rhiannon's circle.

Rhiannon's ring of dark force expanded relentlessly, out and out, and where it touched the Dhuvians the cold ophidian bodies withered and shriveled and lay like cast-off skins upon the stones.

Rhiannon spoke no more. Carse felt the deadly throb of power in his hand as the shining wheel spun faster and faster on its mount and his mind shuddered away from what he could sense in Rhiannon's mind.

For he could sense dimly the nature of the Cursed One's terrible weapon. It was akin to that deadly ultra-violet radiation of the Sun which would destroy all life were it not for the shielding ozone in the atmosphere.

But where the ultra-violet radiation known to Carse's Earth science was easily absorbed, that of Rhiannon's ancient alien science lay in uncharted octaves below the four-hundred angstrom limit and could be produced as an expanding halo that no matter could absorb. And where it touched living tissue, it killed.

Carse hated the Dhuvians but never in the world had there been such hatred in a human heart as he felt now in Rhiannon.

Garach began to whimper. Whimpering, he recoiled from the blazing eyes of the man who towered above him. Half scrambling, half running, he darted away with a sound like laughter in his throat.

Straight out into the dark ring he ran and death received him and silently withered him.

Spreading, spreading, the silent force pulsed outward. Through metal and flesh and stone it went, withering, killing, hunting down the last child of the Serpent who fled through the dark corridors of Caer Dhu. No more weapons flamed against it. No more supple arms were raised to fend it off.

It struck the enclosing Veil at last. Carse felt the subtle shock of it checking and then Rhiannon stopped the wheel.

There was a time of utter silence as those three who were left alive in the city stood motionless, too stunned almost to breathe.

LEIGH BRACKETT

At last the voice of Rhiannon spoke. *"The Serpent is dead. Let his city—and my weapons that have wrought such evil in this world—pass with the Dhuvians."*

He turned from the crystal wheel and sought another instrument, one of the squat looped metal rods.

He raised the small black thing and pressed a secret spring and from the leaden tube that formed its muzzle came a little spark, too bright for the eye to look upon.

Only a tiny fleck of light that settled on the stones. But it began to glow. It seemed to feed on the atoms of the rock as flame feeds on wood. Like wildfire it leaped across the flags. It touched the crystal wheel and the weapon that had destroyed the Serpent was itself consumed.

A chain-reaction such as no nuclear scientist of Earth had conceived, one that could make the atoms of metal and crystal and stone as unstable as the high-number radioactive elements.

Rhiannon said, *"Come."*

They walked through the empty corridors in silence and behind them the strange witchfire fed and fattened and the vast central hall was enveloped in its swift destruction.

The knowledge of Rhiannon guided Carse to the nerve-center of the Veil, to a chamber by the great gate, there to set the controls so that the glimmering web was forever darkened.

They passed out of the citadel and went back down the broken causeway to the quay where the black barge floated.

Then they turned, and looked back, upon the destruction of a city.

They shielded their eyes, for the strange and awful blaze had something in it of the fire of the Sun. It had raced hungrily outward through the sprawling ruins, and made of the central keep a torch that lighted all the sky, blotting out the stars, paling the low moons.

The causeway began to burn, a lengthening tongue of flame between the reeds of the marshland.

Rhiannon raised the squat looped tube again. From it, now, a dim little globule of light not a spark, flew toward the nearing blaze.

And the blaze hesitated, wavered, then began to dull and die.

The witchfire of strange atomic reaction that Rhiannon had triggered he had now damped and killed by some limiting counter-factor whose nature Carse could not dream.

They poled the barge out onto the water as the quivering radiance behind them sank and died. And then the night was dark again and of Caer Dhu there was nothing to be seen but steam.

The voice of Rhiannon spoke, once more. *"It is done,"* he said. *"I have redeemed my sin."*

The Earthman felt the utter weariness of the being within him as the possession was withdrawn from his brain and body.

And then, again, he was only Matthew Carse.

CHAPTER NINETEEN
Judgment of the Quiru

THE WHOLE WORLD seemed hushed and still in the dawn as their barge went down to Sark. None of them spoke and none of them looked back at the vast white steam that still rolled solemnly up across the sky.

Carse felt numbed, drained of all emotion. He had let the wrath of Rhiannon use him and he could not yet feel quite the same. He knew that there was something of it still in his face, for the other two would not quite meet his eyes nor did they break the silence.

The great crowd gathered on the waterfront of Sark was silent too. It seemed that they had stood there for long looking toward Caer Dhu, and even now, after the glare of its destruction had died out of the sky, they stared with white, frightened faces.

Carse looked out at the Khond longships riding with their sails slack against the yards and knew that that terrible blaze had awed the Sea Kings into waiting.

The black barge glided in to the palace stair. The crowd surged forward as Ywain stepped ashore, their voices rising in a strange hushed clamor. And Ywain spoke to them.

"Caer Dhu and the Serpent both are gone—destroyed by the Lord Rhiannon."

She turned instinctively toward Carse. And the eyes of all that vast throng dwelt upon him as the word spread, growing at last to an overwhelming cry of thankfulness.

"Rhiannon! Rhiannon the Deliverer!"

He was the Cursed One no longer, at least not to these Sarks. And for the first time, Carse realized the loathing they had had for the allies Garach had forced upon them.

He walked toward the palace with Ywain and Boghaz and knew with a sense of awe how it felt to be a god. They entered the dim cool halls and it seemed already as though a shadow had gone out of them. Ywain paused at the doors of the throne room as though she had just remembered that she was ruler now in Garach's place.

She turned to Carse and said, "If the Sea Kings still attack . . ."

"They won't—not until they know what happened. And now we must find Rold if he still lives."

"He lives," said Ywain. "After the Dhuvians emptied Rold of his knowledge my father held him as hostage for me."

They found the Lord of Khondor at last, chained in the dungeons deep under the palace walls. He was wasted and drawn with suffering but he still had the spirit left to raise his red head and snarl at Carse and Ywain.

"Demon," he said. "Traitor. Have you and your hellcat come at last to kill me?"

Carse told him the story of Caer Dhu and Rhiannon, watching Rold's expression change slowly from savage despair to a stunned and unbelieving joy.

"Your fleet stands off Sark under Ironbeard," he finished. "Will you take this word to the Sea Kings and bring them in to parley?"

"Aye," said Rold. "By the gods I will!" He stared at Carse, shaking his head. "A strange dream of madness these last days have been! And now—to think that I would have slain you gladly in the place of the Wise Ones with my own hand!"

That was shortly after dawn. By noon the council of the Sea Kings was assembled in the throne room with Rold at their head and Emer, who had refused to stay behind in Khondor.

They sat around a long table. Ywain occupied the throne and Carse stood apart from all of them. His face was stern and very weary and there was in it still a hint of strangeness.

He said with finality, "There need be no war now. The Serpent is gone and without its power Sark can no longer oppress her neighbors. The subject cities, like Jekkara and Valkis, will be freed. The empire of Sark is no more."

Ironbeard leaped to his feet, crying fiercely. "Then now is our chance to destroy Sark forever!"

Others of the Sea Kings rose, Thorn of Tarak loud among them, shouting their assent. Ywain's hand tightened upon her sword.

Carse stepped forward, his eyes blazing. "I say there will be peace! Must I call upon Rhiannon to enforce my word?"

They quieted, awed by that threat, and Rold bade them sit and hold their tongues.

"There has been enough of fighting and bloodshed," he told them sternly. "And for the future we can meet Sark on equal terms. I am Lord of Khondor and I say that Khondor will make peace!"

Caught between Carse's threat and Rold's decision the Sea Kings one by one agreed. Then Emer spoke. "The slaves must all be freed—human and Halfling alike."

Carse nodded. "It will be done."

"And," said Rold, "there is another condition." He faced Carse with unalterable determination. "I have said we will make peace with Sark—but not, though you bring fifty Rhiannons against us, with a Sark that is ruled by Ywain!"

"Aye," roared the Sea Kings, looking wolf-eyed at Ywain. "That is our word also."

There was silence then and Ywain rose from the high seat, her face proud and somber.

"The condition is met," she said. "I have no wish to rule over a Sark tamed and stripped of empire. I hated the Serpent as you did—but it is too late for me to be queen of a petty village of fishermen. The people may choose another ruler."

She stepped down from the dais and went from them to stand erect by a window at the far end of the room, looking out over the harbor.

Carse turned to the Sea Kings. "It is agreed, then."

And they answered, "It is agreed."

Emer, whose fey gaze had not wavered from Carse since the beginning of the parley, came to his side now, laying her hand on his. "And where is your place in this?" she asked softly.

Carse looked down at her, rather dazedly. "I have not had time to think."

But it must be thought of, now. And he did not know.

As long as he bore within him the shadow of Rhiannon this world would never accept him as a man. Honor he might have but never anything more and the lurking fear of the Cursed One would remain. Too many centuries of hate had grown around that name.

Rhiannon had redeemed his crime but even so, as long as Mars lived, he would be remembered as the Cursed One.

As though in answer, for the first time since Caer Dhu, the dark invader stirred and his thought-voice whispered in Carse's mind.

"Go back to the Tomb and I will leave you, for I would follow my brothers. After that you are free. I can guide you back along that pathway to your own time if you wish. Or you can remain here."

And still Carse did not know.

He liked this green and smiling Mars. But as he looked at the Sea Kings, who were waiting for his answer, and then beyond them through the windows to the White Sea and the marshes, it came to him that this was not his world, that he could never truly belong to it.

He spoke at last and as he did so he saw Ywain's face turned toward him in the shadows.

"Emer knew and the Halflings also that I was not of your world. I came out of space and time, along the pathway which is hidden in the Tomb of Rhiannon."

He paused to let them grasp that and they did not seem greatly astonished. Because of what had happened they could believe anything of him, even though it be beyond their comprehension.

Carse said heavily, "A man is born into one world and there he belongs. I am quickly going back to my own place."

He could see that even though they protested courteously, the Sea Kings were relieved.

"The blessings of the gods attend you, stranger," Emer whispered and kissed him gently on the lips.

Then she went and the jubilant Sea Kings went with her. Boghaz had slipped out and Carse and Ywain were alone in the great empty room.

He went to her, looking into her eyes that had not lost their old fire even now. "And where will you go now?" he asked her.

She answered quietly, "If you will let me I go with you."

He shook his head. "No. You could not live in my world, Ywain. It's a cruel and bitter place, very old and near to death."

"It does not matter. My own world also is dead."

He put his hands on her shoulders, strong beneath the mailed shirt. "You don't understand. I came a long way across time—a million years." He paused, not quite knowing how to tell her.

"Look out there. Think how it will be when the White Sea is only a desert of blowing dust—when the green is gone from the hills and the white cities are crumbled and the river beds are dry."

Ywain understood and sighed. "Age and death come at last to everything. And death will come very swiftly to me if I remain here. I am outcast and my name is hated even as Rhiannon's."

He knew that she was not afraid of death but was merely using that argument to sway him.

And yet the argument was true.

"Could you be happy," he asked, "with the memory of your own world haunting you at every step?"

"I have never been happy," she answered, "and therefore I shall not miss it." She looked at him fairly. "I will take the risk. Will you?"

His fingers tightened. "Yes," he said huskily. "Yes, I will."

He took her in his arms and kissed her and when she drew back she whispered, with a shyness utterly new in her, "The 'Lord Rhiannon' spoke truly when he taunted me concerning the barbarian." She was silent a moment, then added, "I think which world we dwell in will not matter much, as long as we are together in it."

Days later the black galley pulled into Jekkara harbor, finishing her last voyage under the ensign of Ywain of Sark.

It was a strange greeting she and Carse received there, where the whole city had gathered to see the stranger, who was also the Cursed One, and the Sovereign Lady of Sark, who was no more a sovereign. The crowd kept back at a respectful distance and they cheered the destruction of Caer Dhu and the death of the Serpent. But for Ywain they had no welcome.

Only one man stood on the quay to meet them. It was Boghaz—a very splendid Boghaz, robed in velvet and loaded down with jewels, wearing a golden circlet on his head.

He had vanished out of Sark on the day of the parley on some mission of his own and it seemed that he had succeeded.

He bowed to Carse and Ywain with grandiloquent politeness.

"I have been to Valkis," he said. "It's a free city again—and because of my unparalleled heroism in helping to destroy Caer Dhu I have been chosen king."

He beamed, then added with a confidential grin, "I always did dream of looting a royal treasury!"

"But," Carse reminded him, "it's *your* treasury now."

Boghaz started. "By the gods, it is so!" He drew himself up, waxing suddenly stern. "I see that I shall have to be severe with thieves in Valkis. There will be heavy punishment for any crime against property—especially royal property!"

"And fortunately," said Carse gravely, "you are acquainted with all the knavish tricks of thieves."

"That is true," said Boghaz sententiously. "I have always said that knowledge is a valuable thing. Behold now, how my purely academic studies of the lawless elements will help me to keep my people safe!"

He accompanied them through Jekkara, until they reached the open country beyond, and then he bade them farewell, plucking off a ring which he thrust into Carse's hand. Tears ran down his fat cheeks.

"Wear this, old friend, that you may remember Boghaz, who guided your steps wisely through a strange world."

He turned and stumbled away and Carse watched his fat figure vanish into the streets of the city, where they had first met.

All alone Carse and Ywain made their way into the hills above Jekkara and came at last to the Tomb. They stood together on the rocky ledge, looking out across the wooded hills and the glowing sea, and the distant towers of the city white in the sunlight.

"Are you still sure," Carse asked her, "that you wish to leave all this?"

"I have no place here now," she answered sadly. "I would be rid of this world as it would be rid of me."

She turned and strode without hesitation into the dark tunnel. Ywain the Proud, that not even the gods themselves could break. Carse went with her, holding a lighted torch.

Through the echoing vault and beyond the door marked with the curse of Rhiannon, into the inner chamber, where the torch-light struck against darkness—the utter darkness of that strange aperture in the space-time continuum of the universe.

At that last moment Ywain's face showed fear and she caught the Earthman's hand. The tiny motes swarmed and flickered before them in the gloom of time itself. The voice of Rhiannon spoke to Carse and he stepped forward into the darkness, holding tightly to Ywain's hand.

This time, at first, there was no headlong plunge into nothingness. The wisdom of Rhiannon guided and steadied them. The torch went out. Carse dropped it. His heart pounded and he was blind and deaf in the soundless vortex of force.

Again Rhiannon spoke. *"See now with my mind what your human eyes could not see before!"*

The pulsing darkness cleared in some strange way that had nothing to do with light or sight. Carse looked upon Rhiannon.

His body lay in a coffin of dark crystal, whose inner facets glowed with the subtle force that prisoned him forever as though frozen in the heart of a jewel.

Through the cloudy substance, Carse could make out dimly a naked form of more than human strength and beauty, so vital and instinct with life that it seemed a terrible thing to prison it in that narrow space. The face also was beautiful, dark and imperious and stormy even now with the eyes closed as though in death.

But there could be no death in this place. It was beyond time and without time there is no decay and Rhiannon would have all eternity to lie there, remembering his sin.

While he stared, Carse realized that the alien being had withdrawn from him so gently and carefully that there had been no shock. His mind was still in touch with the mind of Rhiannon but the strange dualism was ended. The Cursed One had released him.

Yet, through that sympathy that still existed between these two minds that had been one for so long, Carse heard Rhiannon's passionate call—a mental cry that pulsed far out along the pathway through space and time.

"My brothers of the Quiru, hear me! I have undone my ancient crime."

Again he called with all the wild strength of his will. There was a period of silence, of nothingness and then, gradually, Carse sensed the approach of other minds, grave and powerful and stern.

He would never know from what far world they had come. Long ago the Quiru had gone out by this road that led beyond the universe, to cosmic regions forever outside his ken. And now they had come back briefly in answer to Rhiannon's call.

Dim and shadowy, Carse saw godlike forms come slowly into being, tenuous as shining smoke in the gloom.

"Let me go with you, my brothers! For I have destroyed the Serpent and my sin is redeemed."

It seemed that the Quiru pondered, searching Rhiannon's heart for truth. Then at last one stepped forward and laid his hand upon the coffin. The subtle fires died within it.

"It is our judgment that Rhiannon may go free."

A giddiness came over Carse. The scene began to fade. He saw Rhiannon rise and go to join his brothers of the Quiru, his body growing shadowy as he passed.

He turned once to look at Carse, and his eyes were open now, full of a joy beyond human understanding.

"Keep my sword, Earthman—bear it proudly, for without you I could never have destroyed Caer Dhu."

Dizzy, half fainting, Carse received the last mental command. And as he staggered with Ywain through the dark vortex, falling now with nightmare swiftness through the eerie gloom, he heard the last ringing echo of Rhiannon's farewell.

CHAPTER TWENTY
The Return

THERE WAS SOLID rock under their feet at last. They crept trembling away from the vortex, white-faced and shaken, saying nothing, wanting only to be free of that dark vault.

Carse found the tunnel. But when he reached the end he was oppressed by a dread that he might be once again lost in time, and dared not look out.

He need not have feared. Rhiannon had guided them surely. He stood again among the barren hills of his own Mars. It was sunset, and the vast reaches of the dead sea bottom were flooded with the full red light. The wind came cold and dry out of the desert, blowing the dust, and there was Jekkara in the distance—his own Jekkara of the Low Canals.

He turned anxiously to Ywain, watching her face as she looked for the first time upon his world. He saw her lips tighten as though over a deep pain.

Then she threw her shoulders back and smiled and settled the hilt of her sword in its sheath.

"Let us go," she said and placed her hand again in his.

They walked the long weary way across the desolate land and the ghosts of the past were all around them. Now, over the bones of Mars, Carse could see the living flesh that had clothed it once in splendor, the tall trees and the rich earth, and he would never forget.

He looked out across the dead sea bottom and knew that all the years of his life he would hear the booming roll of surf on the shores of a spectral ocean.

Darkness came. The little low moons rose in the cloudless sky. Ywain's hand was firm and strong in his. Carse was aware of a great happiness rising within him. His steps quickened.

They came into the streets of Jekkara, the crumbling street beside the Low Canal. The dry wind shook the torches and the sound of the Harps was as he remembered and the little dark women made tinkling music as they walked.

Ywain smiled. "It is still Mars," she said.

They walked together through the twisting ways—the man who still bore in his face the dark shadow of a god and the woman who had been a queen. The people drew apart to let them pass, staring after them in wonder, and the sword of Rhiannon was like a scepter in Carse's hand.

FOR MORE GREAT LEIGH BRACKETT ADVENTURES, DON'T MISS *THE GINGER STAR* AND *THE SECRET OF SINHARAT!*

Available now from Planet Stories!

ABOUT THE AUTHOR

Leigh Douglass Brackett (1915–1978) was one of the most prominent science fiction authors of her time, equally adept in both crime fiction and westerns. While many of her early stories, beginning with "Martian Quest" in 1940, were science fantasy adventures, her first novel, *No Good from a Corpse* (1944), was a hard-boiled detective mystery that so impressed director Howard Hawks that he had his staff call in "this guy Brackett" to help William Faulkner write the script for *The Big Sleep*. The film, starring Humphrey Bogart and Lauren Bacall, is considered a shining example of film noir, and launched Brackett's scriptwriting career, which would go on to include such notable pictures as *Rio Bravo*, *The Long Goodbye*, and the first draft of *The Empire Strikes Back*, which was written shortly before her death and later revised significantly. During this time, however, she maintained her status as a pulp science fiction icon, writing numerous stories and occasionally collaborating with protégé Ray Bradbury or husband Edmond Hamilton. Despite her death from cancer in 1978, Brackett's works live on today as some of the most important in the genre.

Collect all of these exciting Planet Stories adventures!

THE SECRET OF SINHARAT
BY LEIGH BRACKETT
INTRODUCTION BY MICHAEL MOORCOCK

In the Martian Drylands, a criminal conspiracy leads wild man Eric John Stark to a secret that could shake the Red Planet to its core. In a bonus novel, *People of the Talisman*, Stark ventures to the polar ice cap of Mars to return a stolen talisman to an oppressed people.

ISBN: 978-1-60125-047-6

THE GINGER STAR
BY LEIGH BRACKETT
INTRODUCTION BY BEN BOVA

Eric John Stark journeys to the dying world of Skaith in search of his kidnapped foster father, only to find himself the subject of a revolutionary prophecy. In completing his mission, will he be forced to fulfill the prophecy as well?

ISBN: 978-1-60125-084-1

THE HOUNDS OF SKAITH
BY LEIGH BRACKETT
INTRODUCTION BY F. PAUL WILSON

Eric John Stark has destroyed the Citadel of the Lords Protector, but the war for Skaith's freedom is just beginning. Together with his foster father Simon Ashton, Stark will have to unite some of the strangest and most bloodthirsty peoples the galaxy has ever seen if he ever wants to return home.

ISBN: 978-1-60125-135-0

CITY OF THE BEAST
BY MICHAEL MOORCOCK
INTRODUCTION BY KIM MOHAN

Moorcock's Eternal Champion returns as Michael Kane, an American physicist and expert duelist whose strange experiments catapult him through space and time to a Mars of the distant past—and into the arms of the gorgeous princess Shizala. But can he defeat the Blue Giants of the Argzoon in time to win her hand?

ISBN: 978-1-60125-044-5

LORD OF THE SPIDERS
BY MICHAEL MOORCOCK
INTRODUCTION BY ROY THOMAS

Michael Kane returns to the Red Planet, only to find himself far from his destination and caught in the midst of a civil war between giants! Will his wits and wrist keep him alive long enough to find his true love once more?

ISBN: 978-1-60125-082-7

ALMURIC
BY ROBERT E. HOWARD
INTRODUCTION BY JOE R. LANSDALE

From the creator of Conan, Almuric is a savage planet of crumbling stone ruins and debased, near-human inhabitants. Into this world comes Esau Cairn—Earthman, swordsman, murderer. Can one man overthrow the terrible devils that enslave Almuric?

ISBN: 978-1-60125-043-8

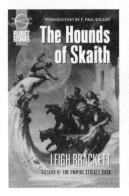  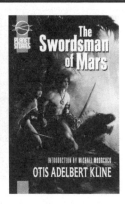